The Championship!

#4

Laurent Richard
illustrated by Nicolas Ryser
Translation: Edward Gauvin

GRAPHIC UNIVERSE™ • MINNEAPOLIS

STORY BY LAURENT RICHARD
ILLUSTRATIONS BY NICOLAS RYSER
COLORING BY STEVAN ROUDAUT
TRANSLATION BY EDWARD GAUVIN

FIRST AMERICAN EDITION PUBLISHED IN 2014 BY GRAPHIC UNIVERSE™.

AU CHAMPIONNAT D'ARTS MARTIAUX BY LAURENT RICHARD AND NICOLAS RYSER © BAYARD ÉDITIONS, 2011
COPYRIGHT © 2014 BY LERNER PUBLISHING GROUP, INC., FOR THE US EDITION

GRAPHIC UNIVERSE™ IS A TRADEMARK OF LERNER PUBLISHING GROUP, INC.

GRAPHIC UNIVERSE™
A DIVISION OF LERNER PUBLISHING GROUP, INC.
241 FIRST AVENUE NORTH
MINNEAPOLIS, MN 55401 USA

FOR READING LEVELS AND MORE INFORMATION,
LOOK UP THIS TITLE AT WWW.LERNERBOOKS.COM.

MAIN BODY TEXT SET IN CCWILDWORDS 8.5/10.5.
TYPEFACE PROVIDED BY FONTOGRAPHER.

LIBRARY OF CONGRESS CATALOGING-IN-PUBLICATION DATA

RICHARD, LAURENT, 1968–
    [AU CHAMPIONNAT D'ARTS MARTIAUX. ENGLISH]
    THE CHAMPIONSHIP! / BY LAURENT RICHARD ; ILLUSTRATED BY NICOLAS RYSER ; TRANSLATION:
EDWARD GAUVIN. – FIRST AMERICAN EDITION.
        P.   CM. – (TAO, THE LITTLE SAMURAI ; #4)
    SUMMARY: THE STUDENTS OF MASTER SNOW'S DOJO ARE EXCITED ABOUT THEIR TRIP TO THE
INTERNATIONAL MARTIAL ARTS CHAMPIONSHIP, BUT UPON ARRIVAL TWO OF THE BEST FIGHTERS IN
THE SCHOOL'S HISTORY, HIRO AND JAY, DISAPPEAR.
    ISBN 978-1-4677-2097-7 (LIB. BDG. : ALK. PAPER)
    ISBN 978-1-4677-4661-8 (EBOOK)
    1. GRAPHIC NOVELS. [1. GRAPHIC NOVELS. 2. MARTIAL ARTS–FICTION. 3. SAMURAI–FICTION.
4. KIDNAPPING–FICTION. 5. ROBBERS AND OUTLAWS–FICTION.] I. RYSER, NICOLAS, ILLUSTRATOR.
II. GAUVIN, EDWARD, TRANSLATOR. III. TITLE.
PZ7.7.R5CH 2014
741.5'944–DC23   2013038066

MANUFACTURED IN THE UNITED STATES OF AMERICA
1 - VI – 7/15/14

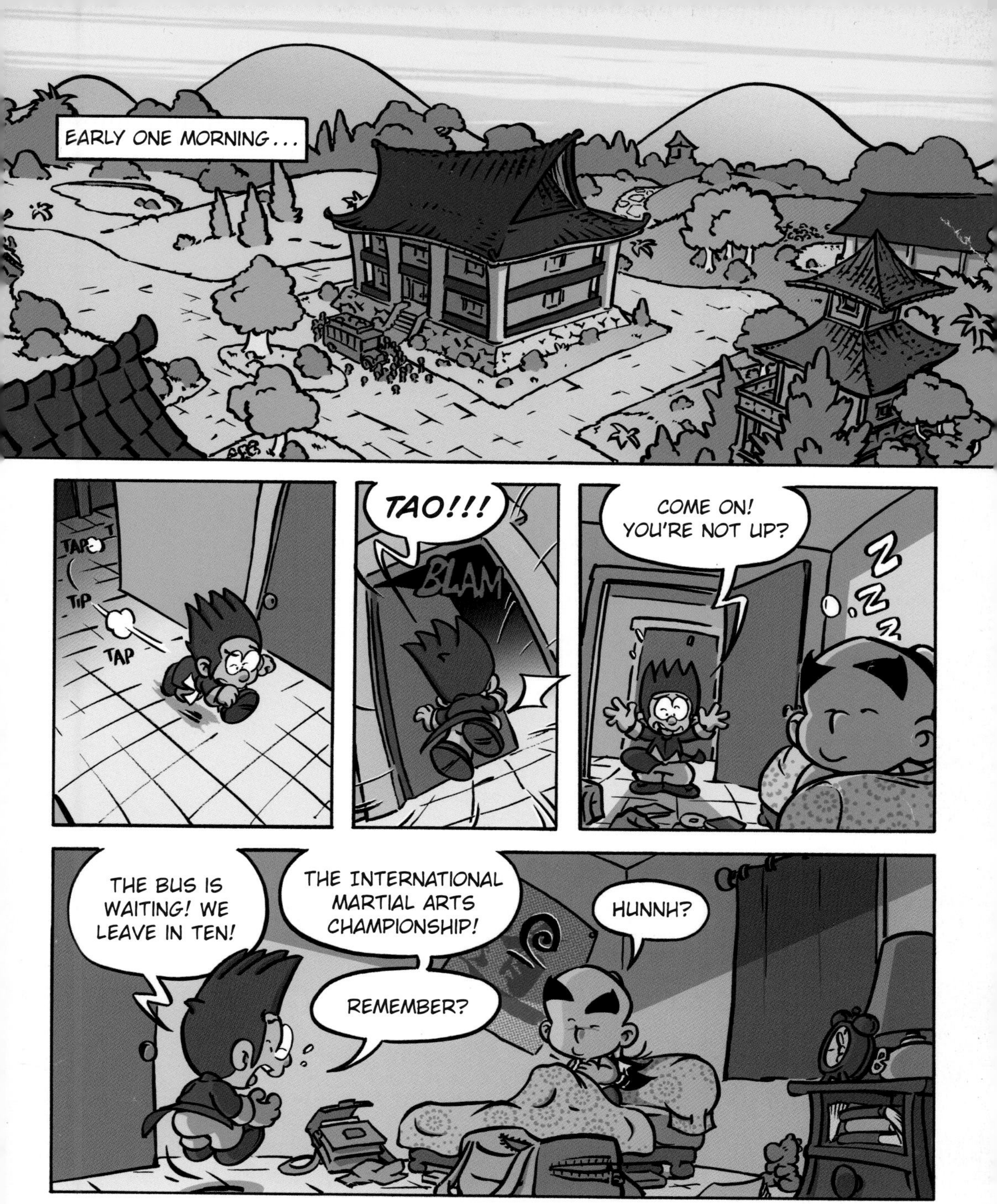
EARLY ONE MORNING...
TAP
TIP
TAP
TAO!!!
BLAM
COME ON! YOU'RE NOT UP?
Z Z Z
THE BUS IS WAITING! WE LEAVE IN TEN!
THE INTERNATIONAL MARTIAL ARTS CHAMPIONSHIP!
REMEMBER?
HUNNH?

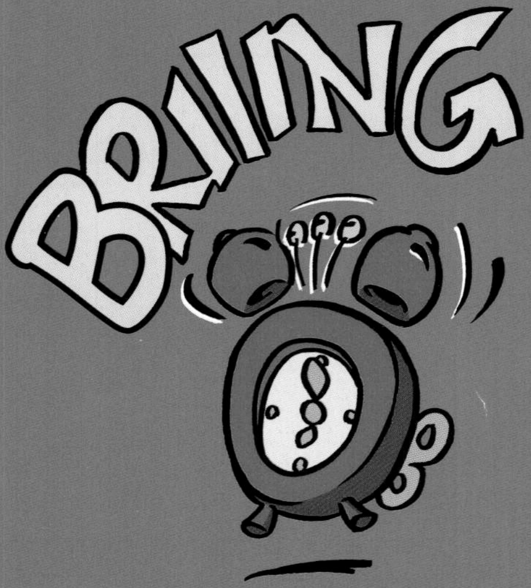
BRIING

Let's
GO!

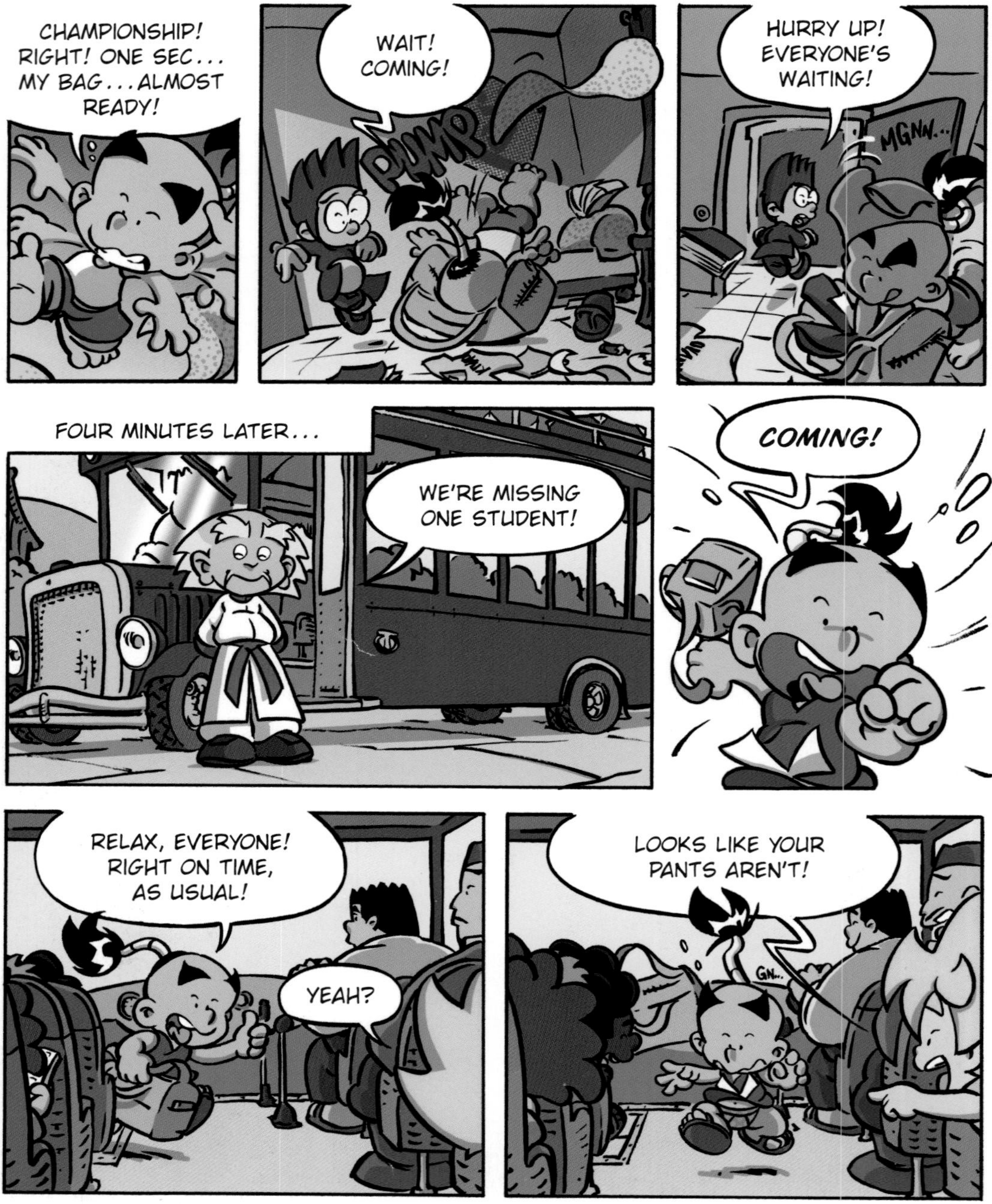
CHAMPIONSHIP! RIGHT! ONE SEC... MY BAG...ALMOST READY!
WAIT! COMING!
PUMP
HURRY UP! EVERYONE'S WAITING!
MGNN...
FOUR MINUTES LATER...
WE'RE MISSING ONE STUDENT!
COMING!
RELAX, EVERYONE! RIGHT ON TIME, AS USUAL!
YEAH?
LOOKS LIKE YOUR PANTS AREN'T!
GN...

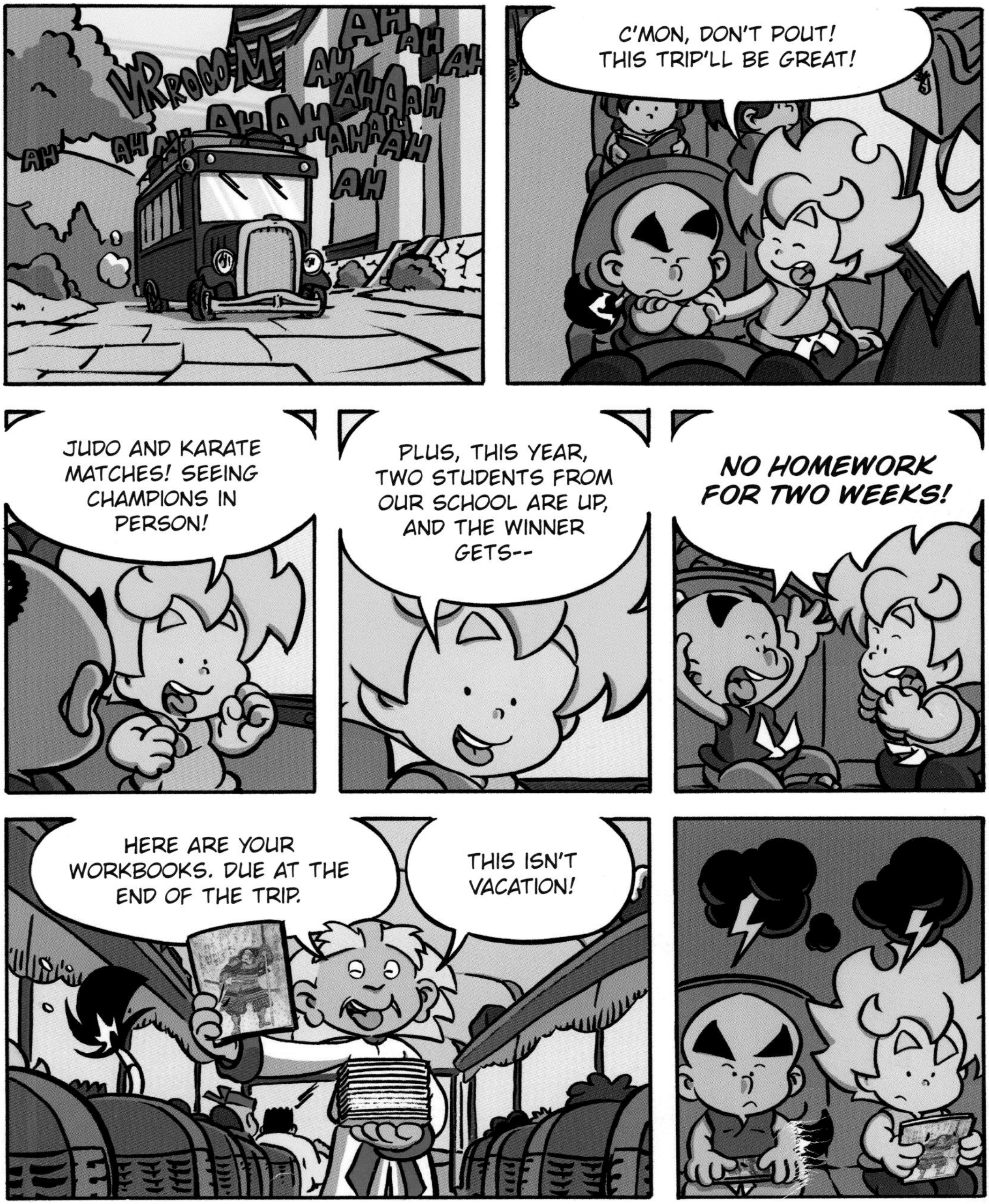
VRROOOM
AH AH AH AH AH
AHAAAH
AH
C'MON, DON'T POUT! THIS TRIP'LL BE GREAT!
JUDO AND KARATE MATCHES! SEEING CHAMPIONS IN PERSON!
PLUS, THIS YEAR, TWO STUDENTS FROM OUR SCHOOL ARE UP, AND THE WINNER GETS--
NO HOMEWORK FOR TWO WEEKS!
HERE ARE YOUR WORKBOOKS. DUE AT THE END OF THE TRIP.
THIS ISN'T VACATION!

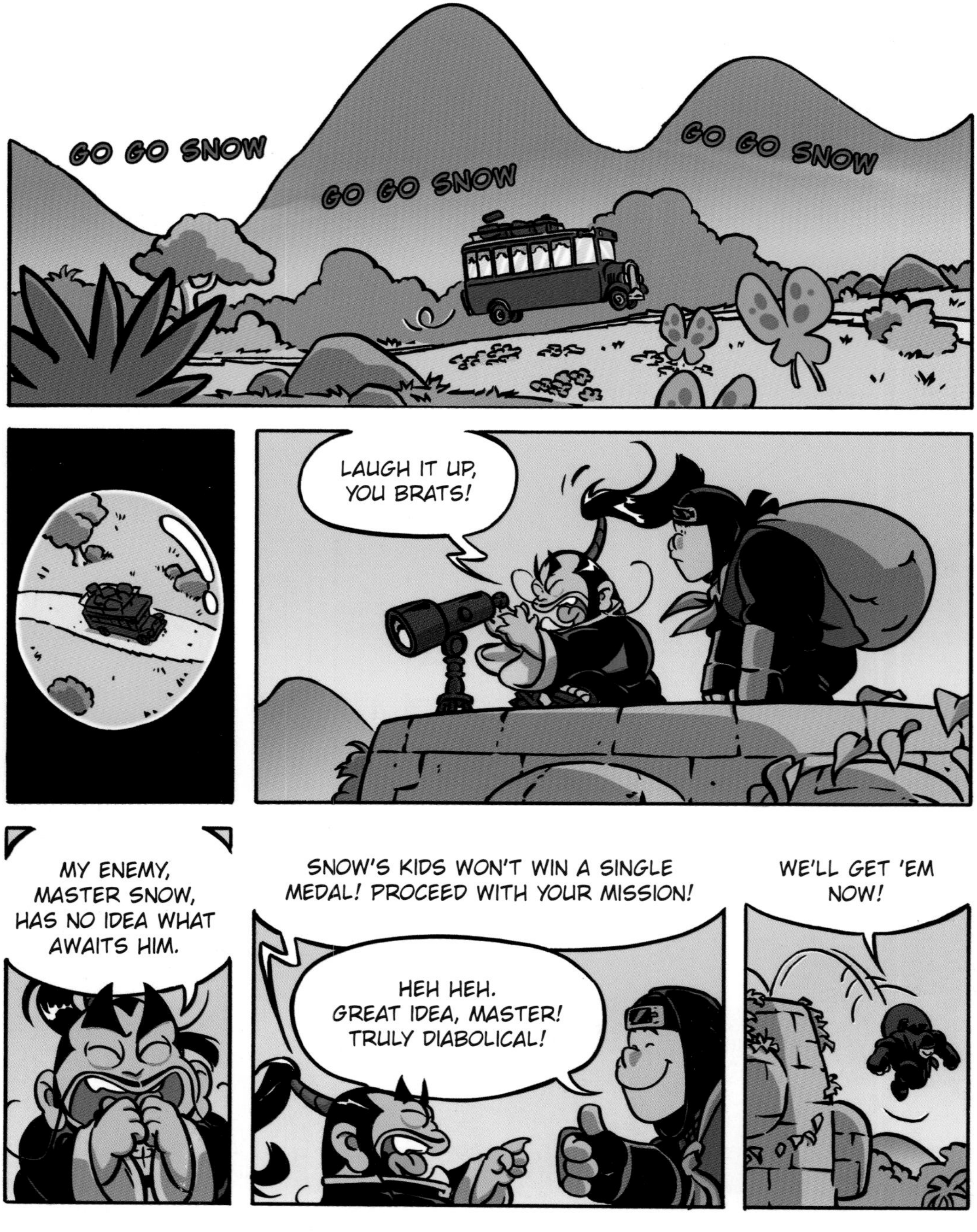
GO GO SNOW
GO GO SNOW
GO GO SNOW
LAUGH IT UP, YOU BRATS!
MY ENEMY, MASTER SNOW, HAS NO IDEA WHAT AWAITS HIM.
SNOW'S KIDS WON'T WIN A SINGLE MEDAL! PROCEED WITH YOUR MISSION!
HEH HEH. GREAT IDEA, MASTER! TRULY DIABOLICAL!
WE'LL GET 'EM NOW!

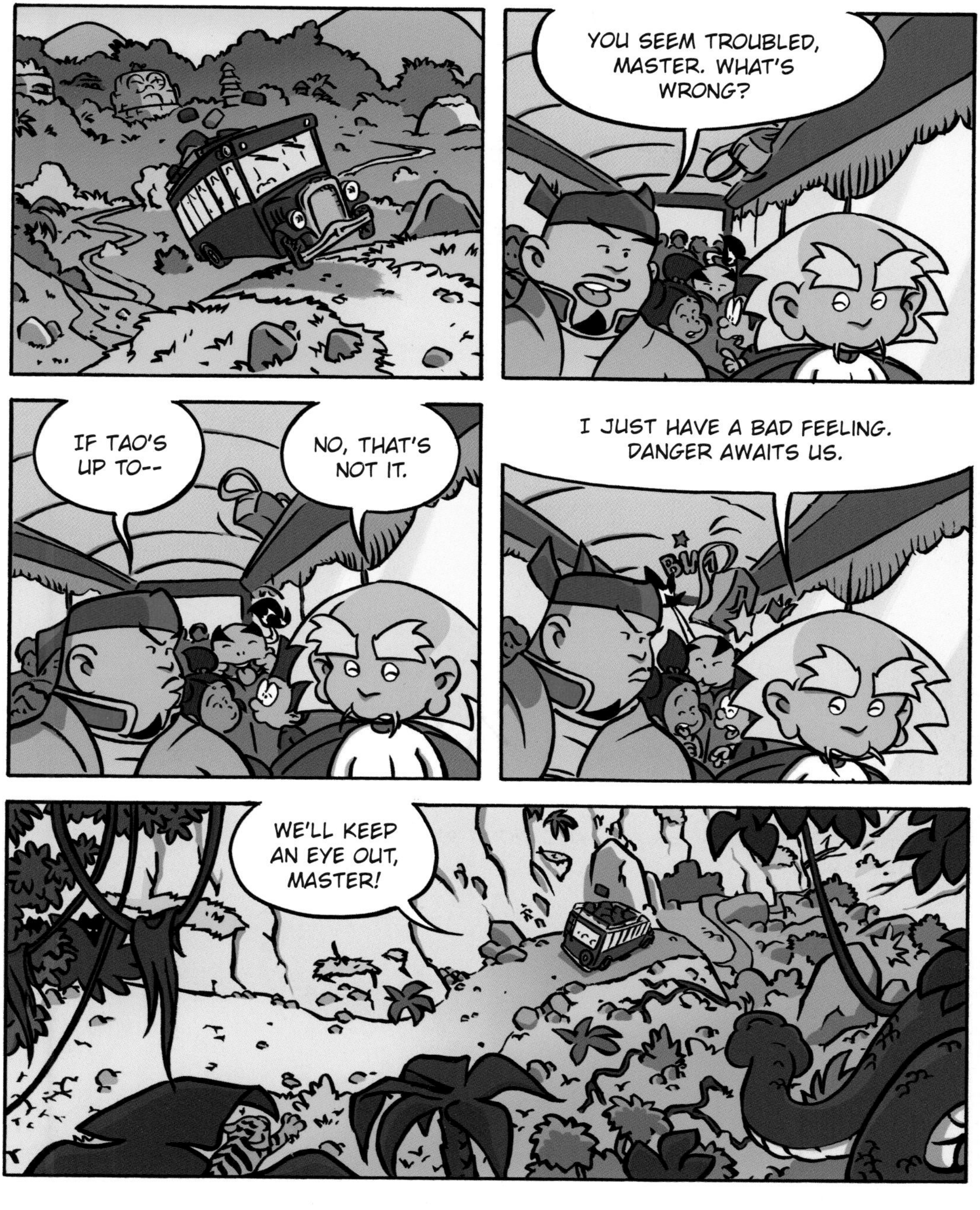
YOU SEEM TROUBLED, MASTER. WHAT'S WRONG?
IF TAO'S UP TO--
NO, THAT'S NOT IT.
I JUST HAVE A BAD FEELING. DANGER AWAITS US.
WE'LL KEEP AN EYE OUT, MASTER!

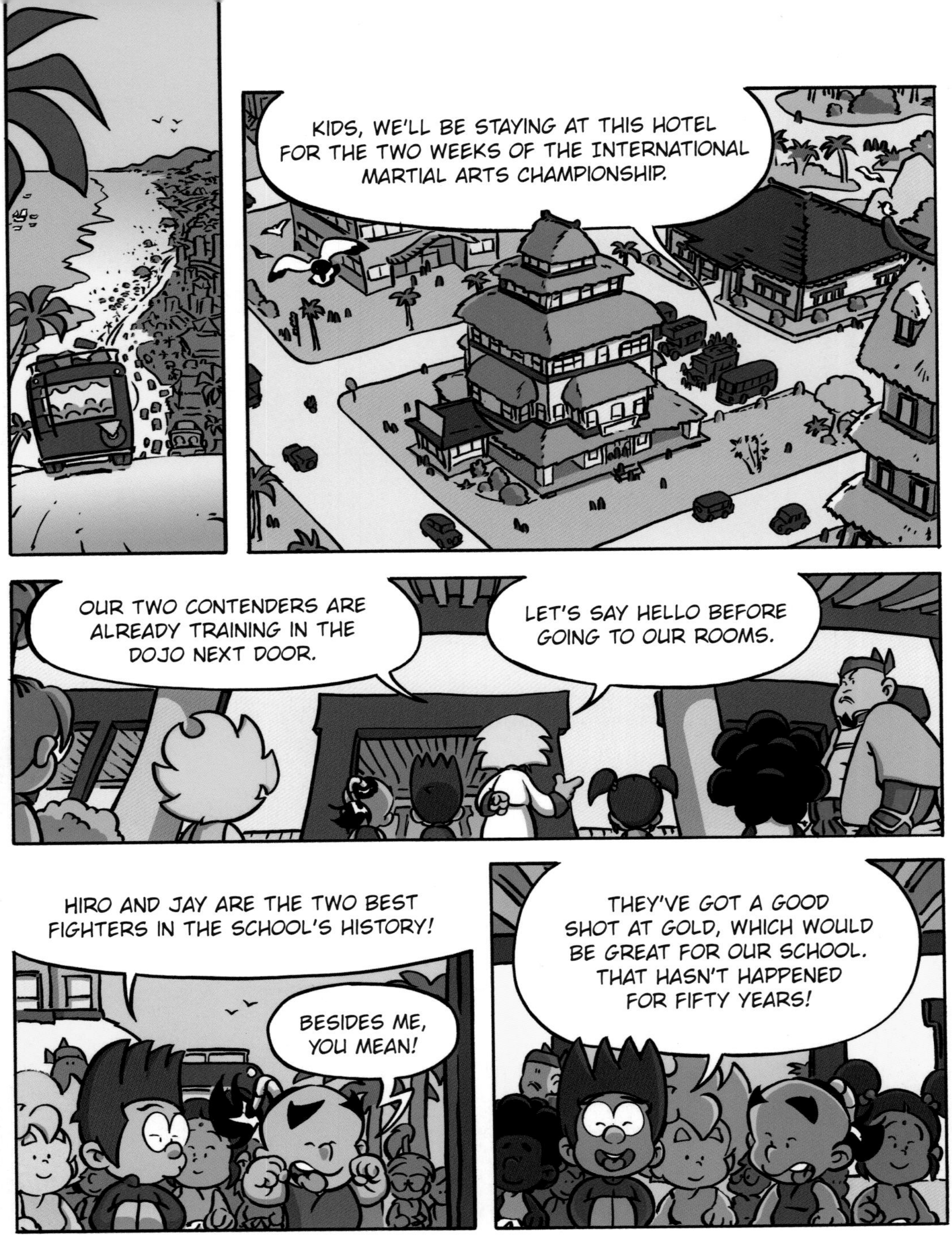

KIDS, WE'LL BE STAYING AT THIS HOTEL FOR THE TWO WEEKS OF THE INTERNATIONAL MARTIAL ARTS CHAMPIONSHIP.
OUR TWO CONTENDERS ARE ALREADY TRAINING IN THE DOJO NEXT DOOR.
LET'S SAY HELLO BEFORE GOING TO OUR ROOMS.
HIRO AND JAY ARE THE TWO BEST FIGHTERS IN THE SCHOOL'S HISTORY!
BESIDES ME, YOU MEAN!
THEY'VE GOT A GOOD SHOT AT GOLD, WHICH WOULD BE GREAT FOR OUR SCHOOL. THAT HASN'T HAPPENED FOR FIFTY YEARS!

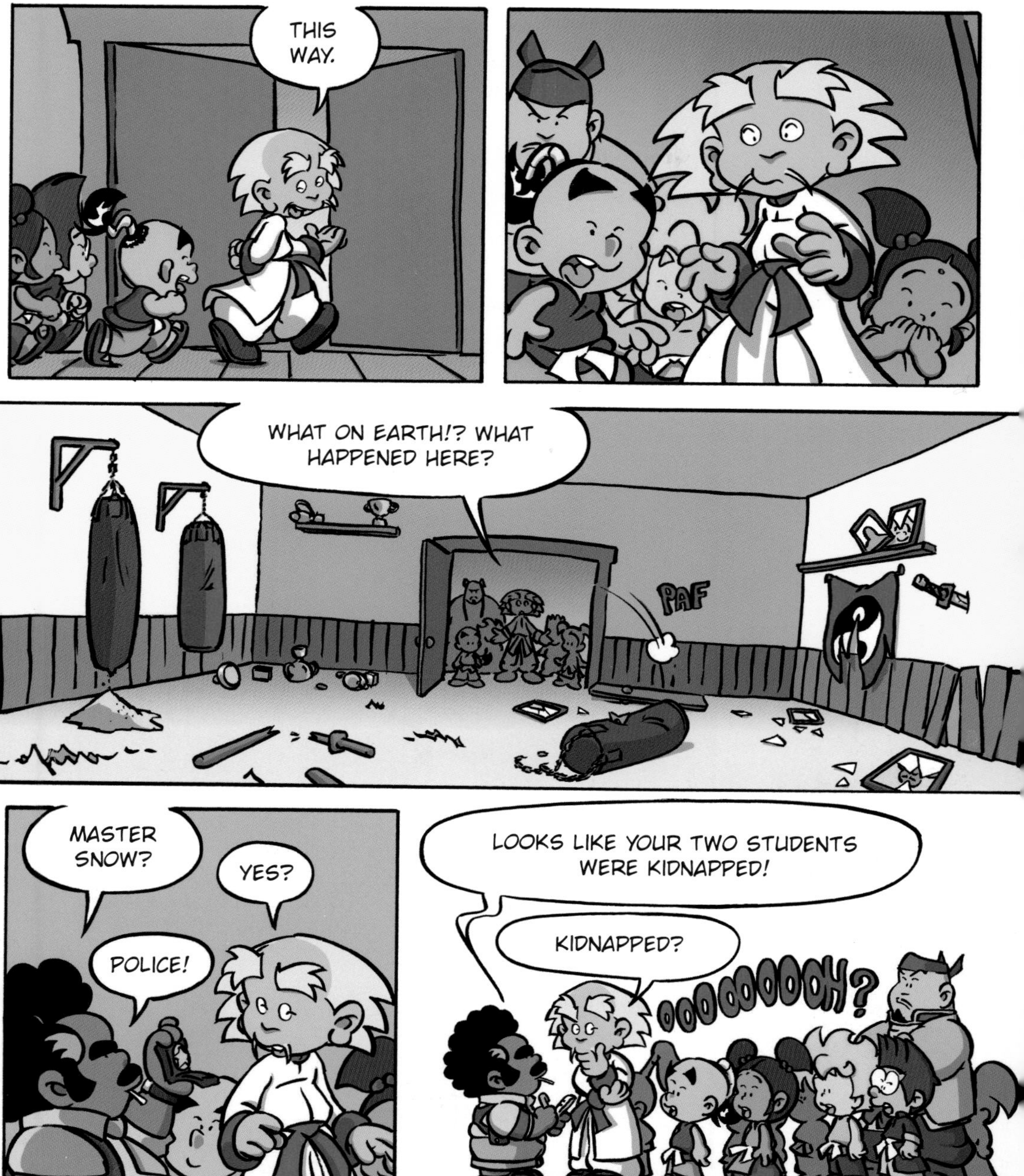
THIS WAY.
WHAT ON EARTH!? WHAT HAPPENED HERE?
PAF
MASTER SNOW?
YES?
POLICE!
LOOKS LIKE YOUR TWO STUDENTS WERE KIDNAPPED!
KIDNAPPED?
OOOOOOOOH?

The Mystery!

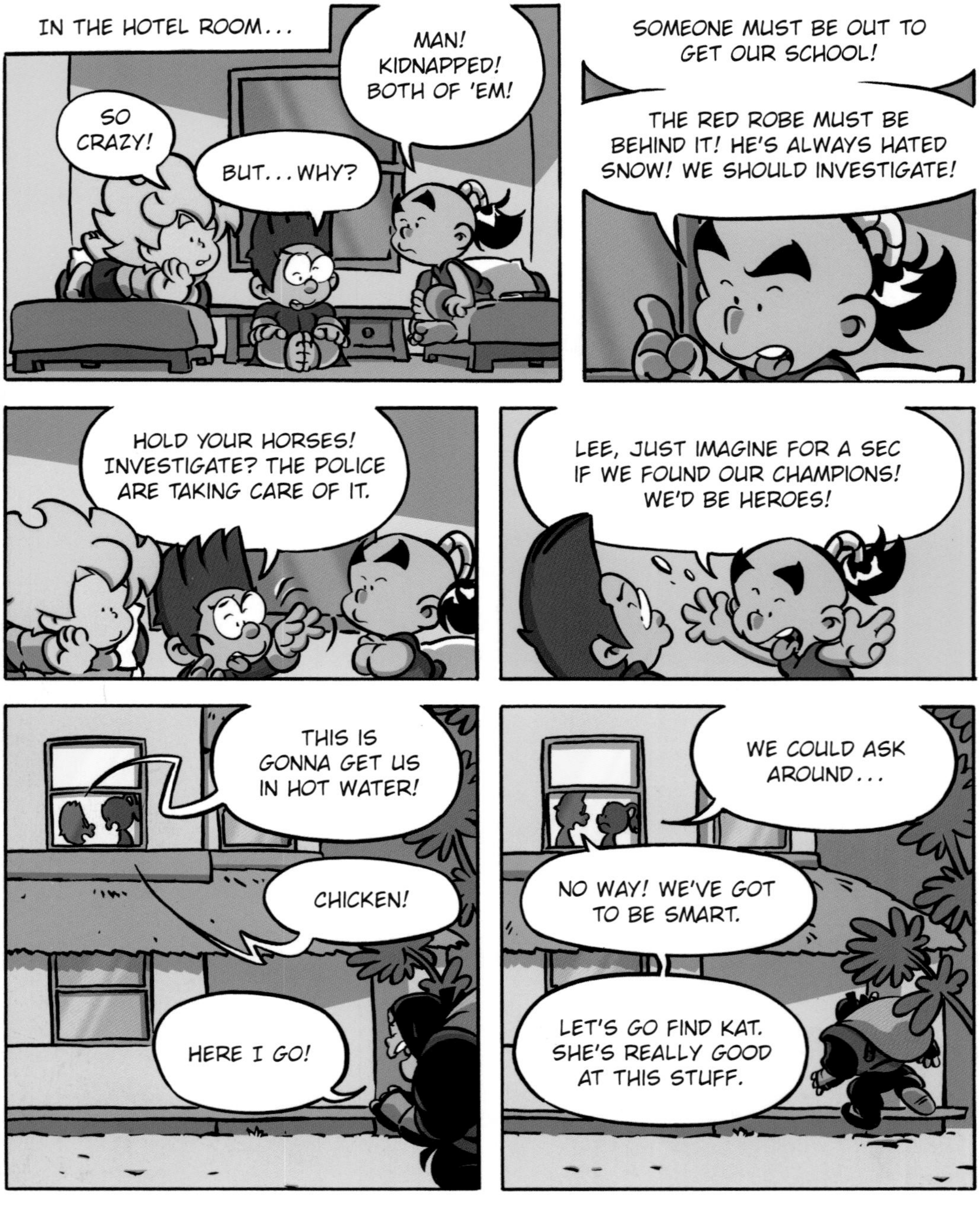
IN THE HOTEL ROOM...
SO CRAZY!
BUT...WHY?
MAN! KIDNAPPED! BOTH OF 'EM!
SOMEONE MUST BE OUT TO GET OUR SCHOOL!
THE RED ROBE MUST BE BEHIND IT! HE'S ALWAYS HATED SNOW! WE SHOULD INVESTIGATE!
HOLD YOUR HORSES! INVESTIGATE? THE POLICE ARE TAKING CARE OF IT.
LEE, JUST IMAGINE FOR A SEC IF WE FOUND OUR CHAMPIONS! WE'D BE HEROES!
THIS IS GONNA GET US IN HOT WATER!
CHICKEN!
HERE I GO!
WE COULD ASK AROUND...
NO WAY! WE'VE GOT TO BE SMART.
LET'S GO FIND KAT. SHE'S REALLY GOOD AT THIS STUFF.

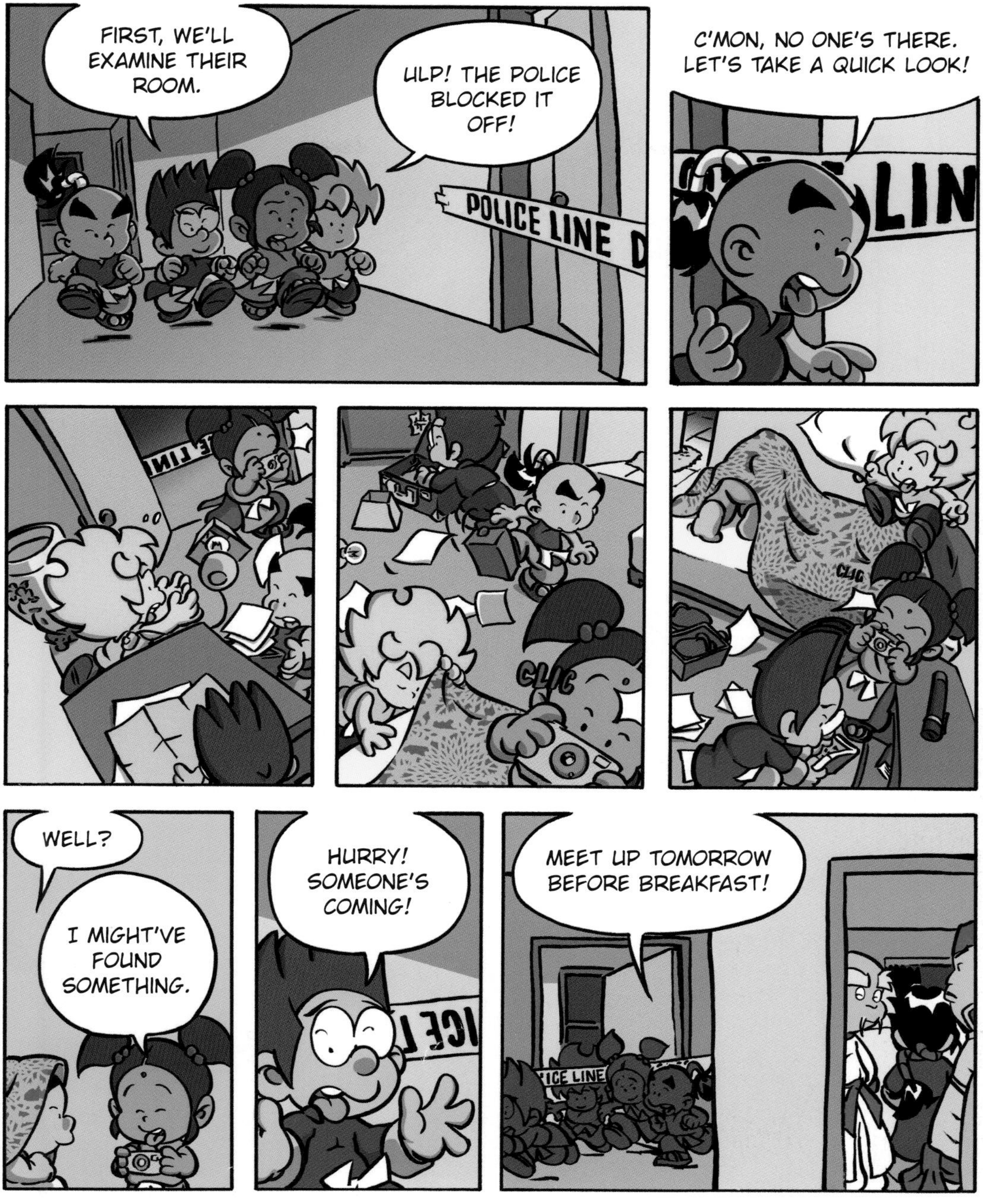
FIRST, WE'LL EXAMINE THEIR ROOM.
ULP! THE POLICE BLOCKED IT OFF!
POLICE LINE D
C'MON, NO ONE'S THERE. LET'S TAKE A QUICK LOOK!
CLIC
CLIC
WELL?
I MIGHT'VE FOUND SOMETHING.
HURRY! SOMEONE'S COMING!
MEET UP TOMORROW BEFORE BREAKFAST!
ICE LINE

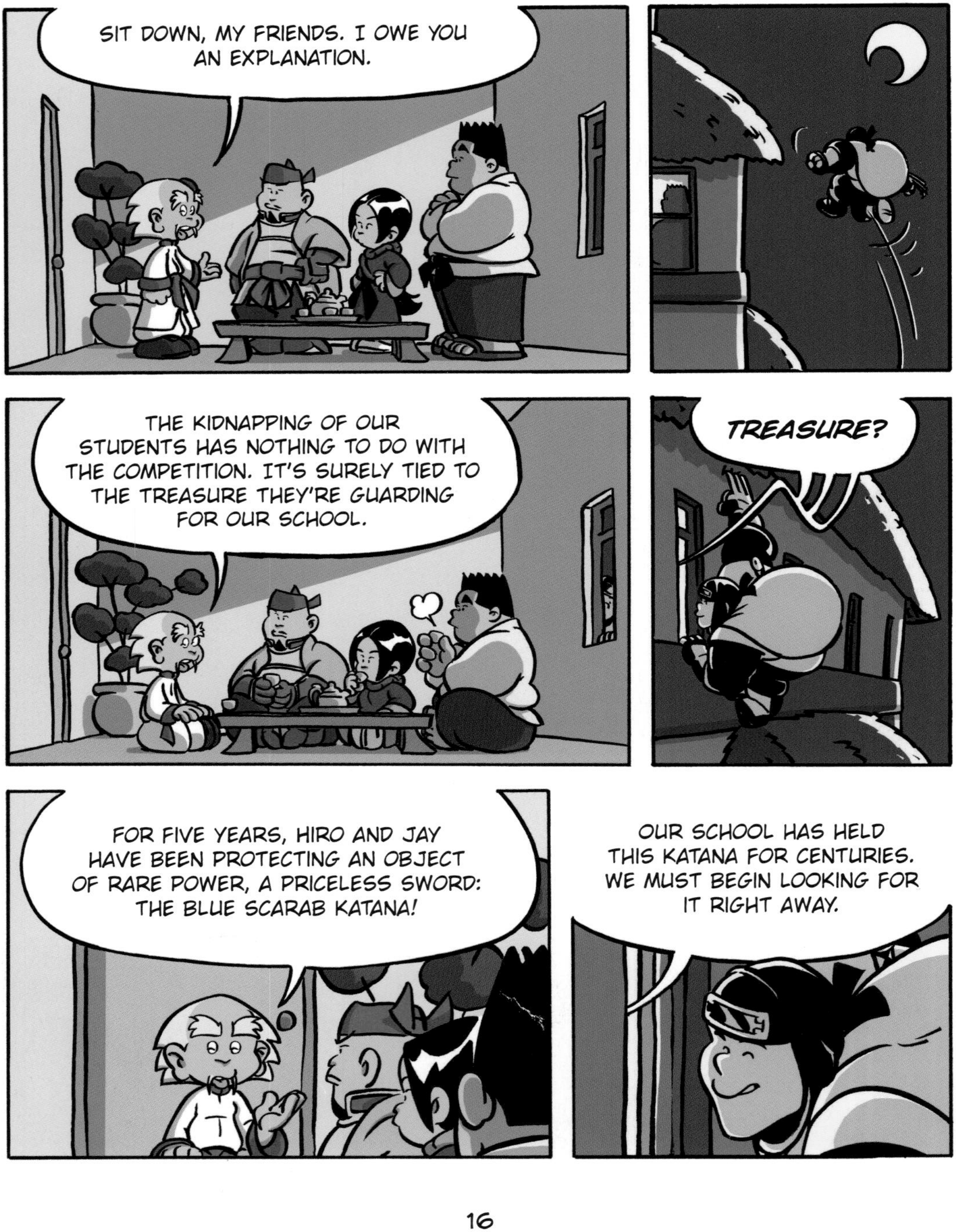
SIT DOWN, MY FRIENDS. I OWE YOU AN EXPLANATION.
THE KIDNAPPING OF OUR STUDENTS HAS NOTHING TO DO WITH THE COMPETITION. IT'S SURELY TIED TO THE TREASURE THEY'RE GUARDING FOR OUR SCHOOL.
TREASURE?
FOR FIVE YEARS, HIRO AND JAY HAVE BEEN PROTECTING AN OBJECT OF RARE POWER, A PRICELESS SWORD: THE BLUE SCARAB KATANA!
OUR SCHOOL HAS HELD THIS KATANA FOR CENTURIES. WE MUST BEGIN LOOKING FOR IT RIGHT AWAY.

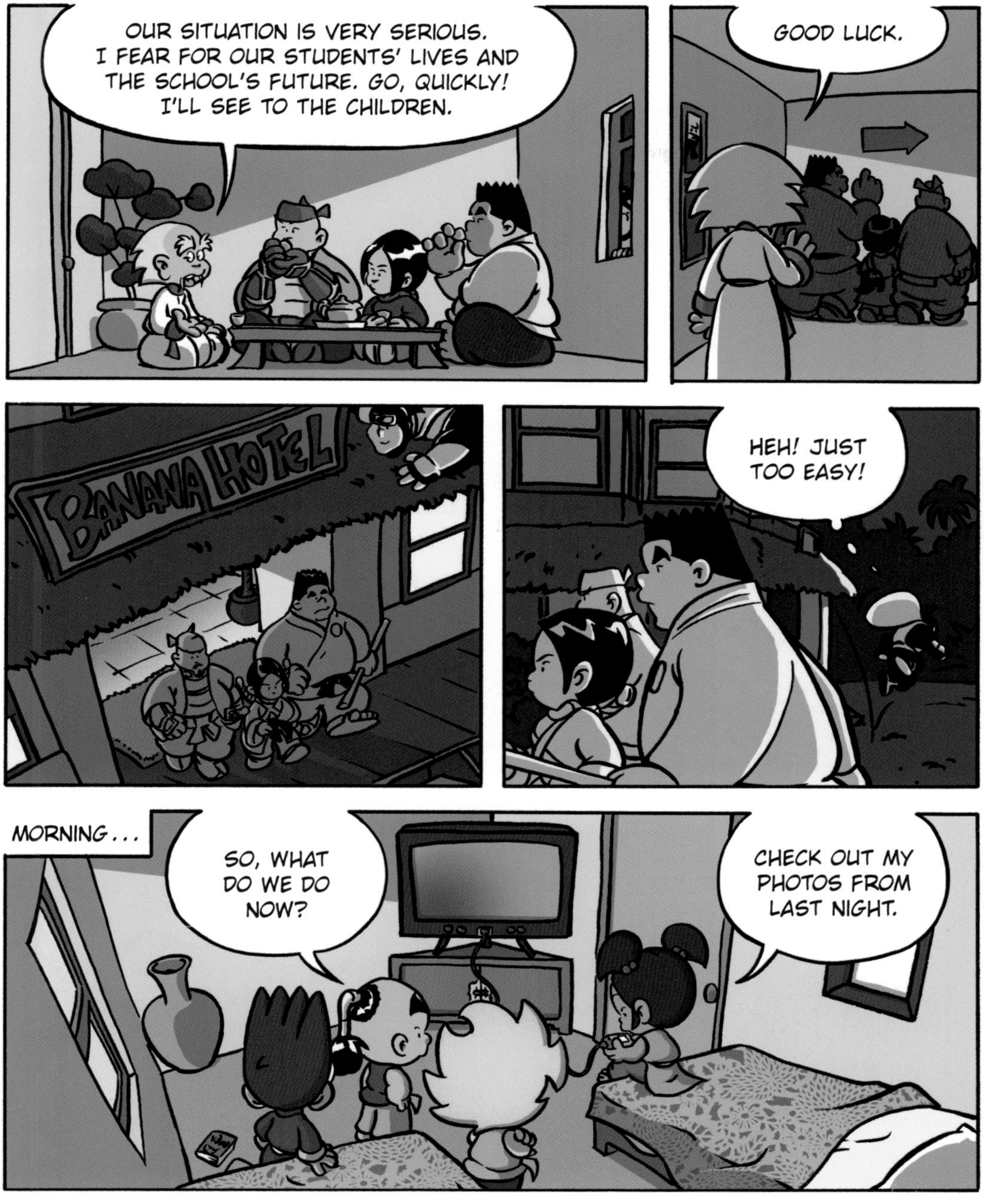

OUR SITUATION IS VERY SERIOUS. I FEAR FOR OUR STUDENTS' LIVES AND THE SCHOOL'S FUTURE. GO, QUICKLY! I'LL SEE TO THE CHILDREN.
GOOD LUCK.
BANANA HOTEL
HEH! JUST TOO EASY!
MORNING . . .
SO, WHAT DO WE DO NOW?
CHECK OUT MY PHOTOS FROM LAST NIGHT.

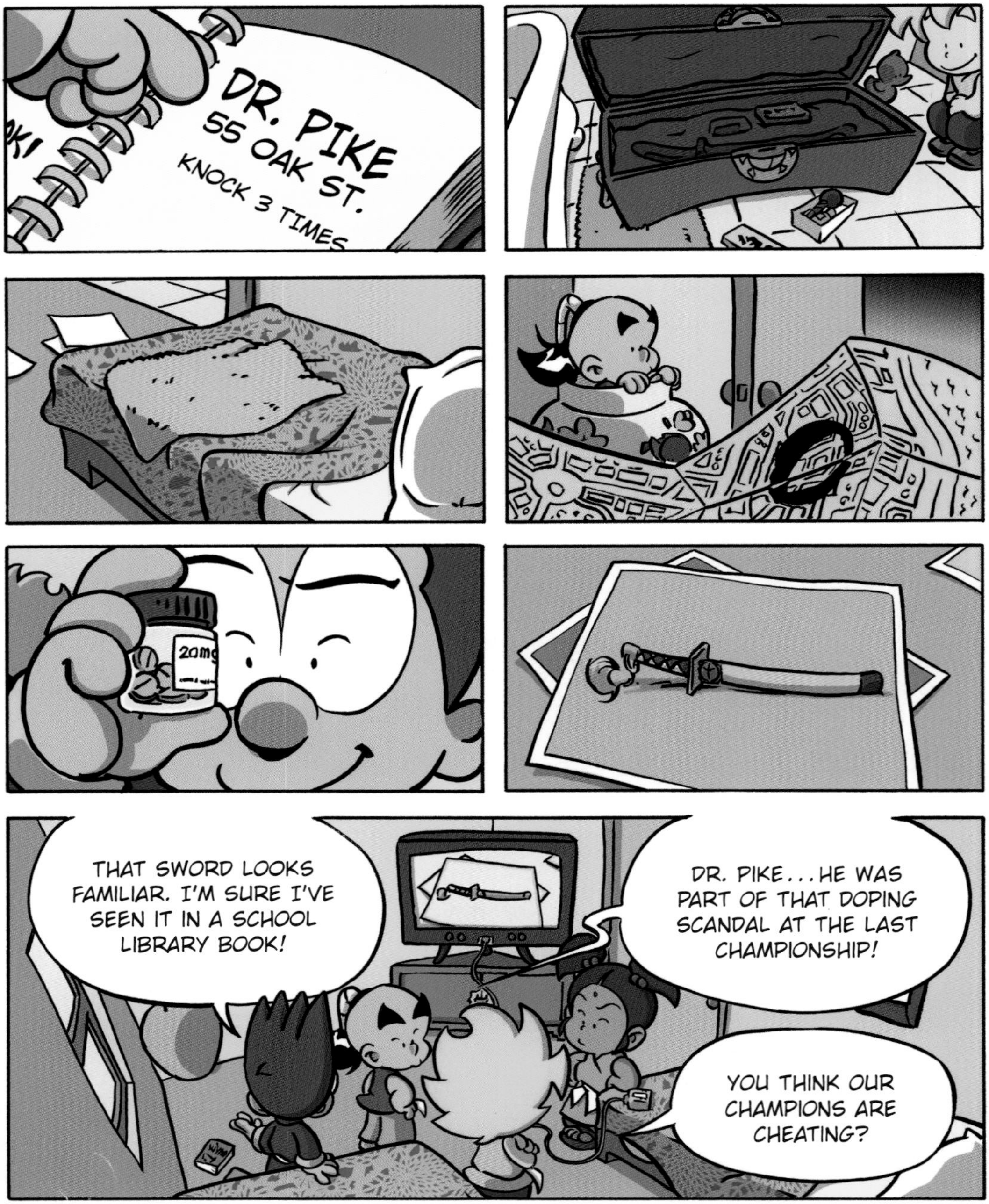
DR. PIKE
55 OAK ST.
KNOCK 3 TIMES
20mg
THAT SWORD LOOKS FAMILIAR. I'M SURE I'VE SEEN IT IN A SCHOOL LIBRARY BOOK!
DR. PIKE . . . HE WAS PART OF THAT DOPING SCANDAL AT THE LAST CHAMPIONSHIP!
YOU THINK OUR CHAMPIONS ARE CHEATING?

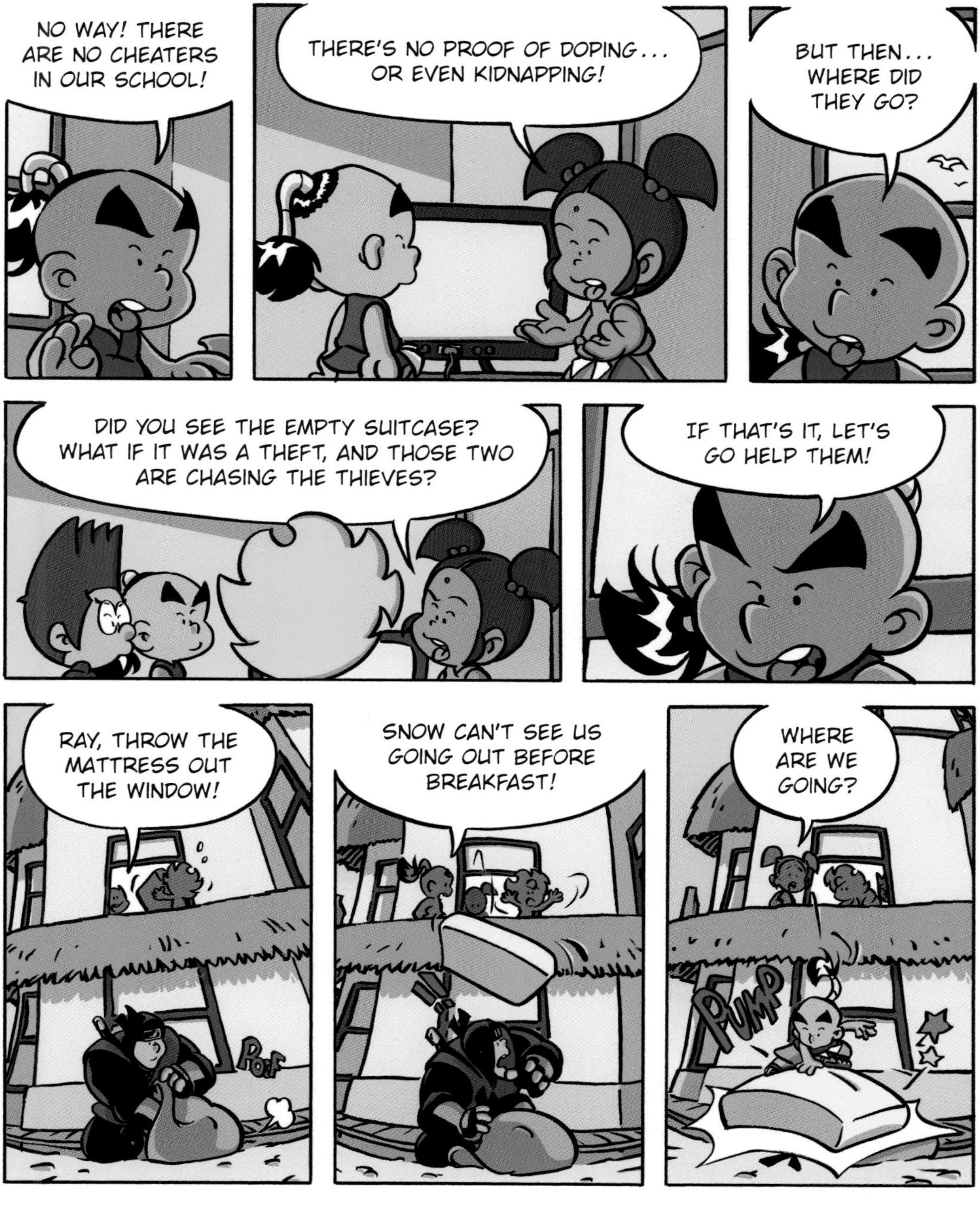
NO WAY! THERE ARE NO CHEATERS IN OUR SCHOOL!
THERE'S NO PROOF OF DOPING... OR EVEN KIDNAPPING!
BUT THEN... WHERE DID THEY GO?
DID YOU SEE THE EMPTY SUITCASE? WHAT IF IT WAS A THEFT, AND THOSE TWO ARE CHASING THE THIEVES?
IF THAT'S IT, LET'S GO HELP THEM!
RAY, THROW THE MATTRESS OUT THE WINDOW!
POF
SNOW CAN'T SEE US GOING OUT BEFORE BREAKFAST!
WHERE ARE WE GOING?
PUMP

The Investigation!

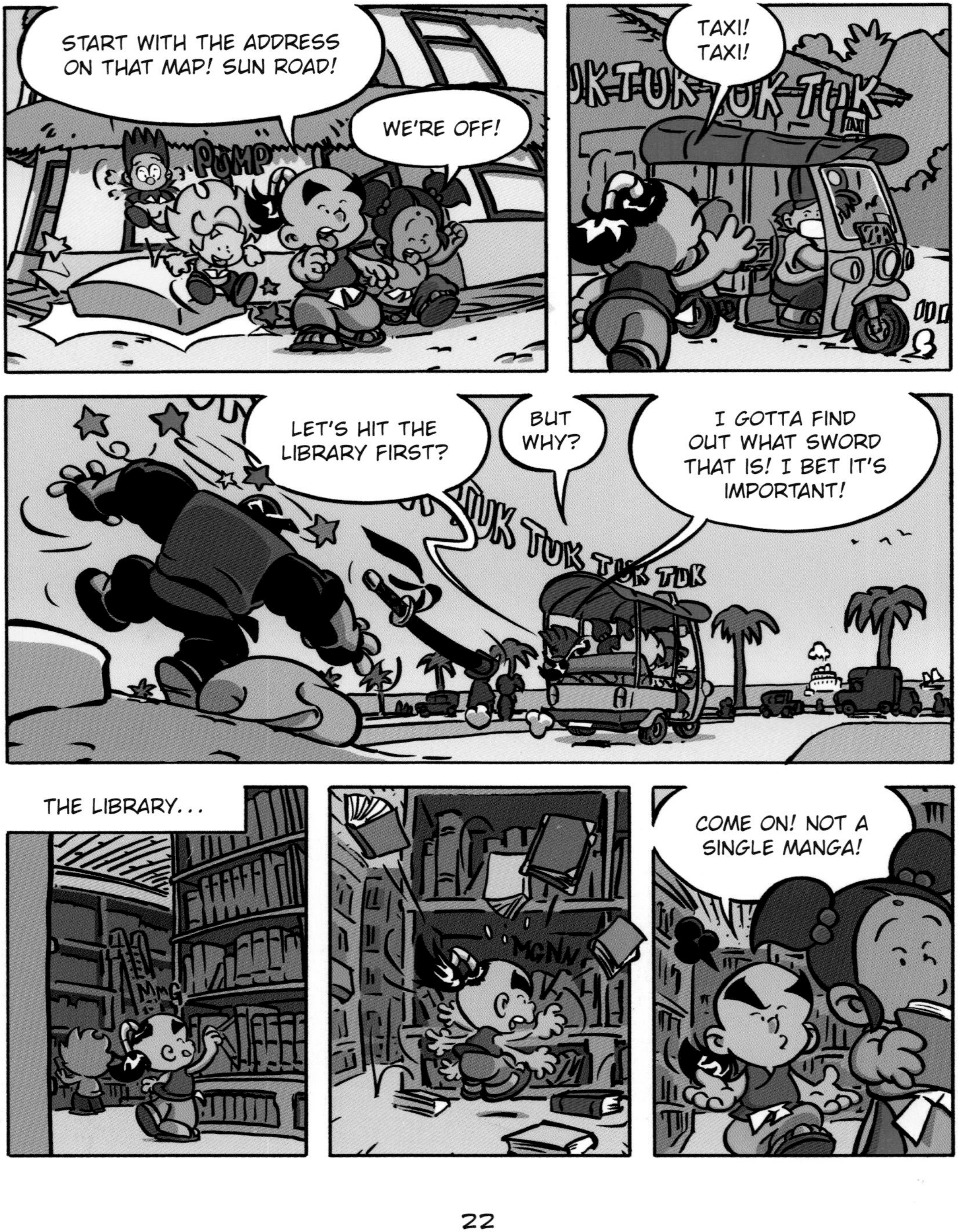
START WITH THE ADDRESS ON THAT MAP! SUN ROAD!
PUMP
WE'RE OFF!
TAXI! TAXI!
TUK TUK TUK TUK
LET'S HIT THE LIBRARY FIRST?
BUT WHY?
I GOTTA FIND OUT WHAT SWORD THAT IS! I BET IT'S IMPORTANT!
TUK TUK TUK TUK
THE LIBRARY...
MMG
MGNN
COME ON! NOT A SINGLE MANGA!

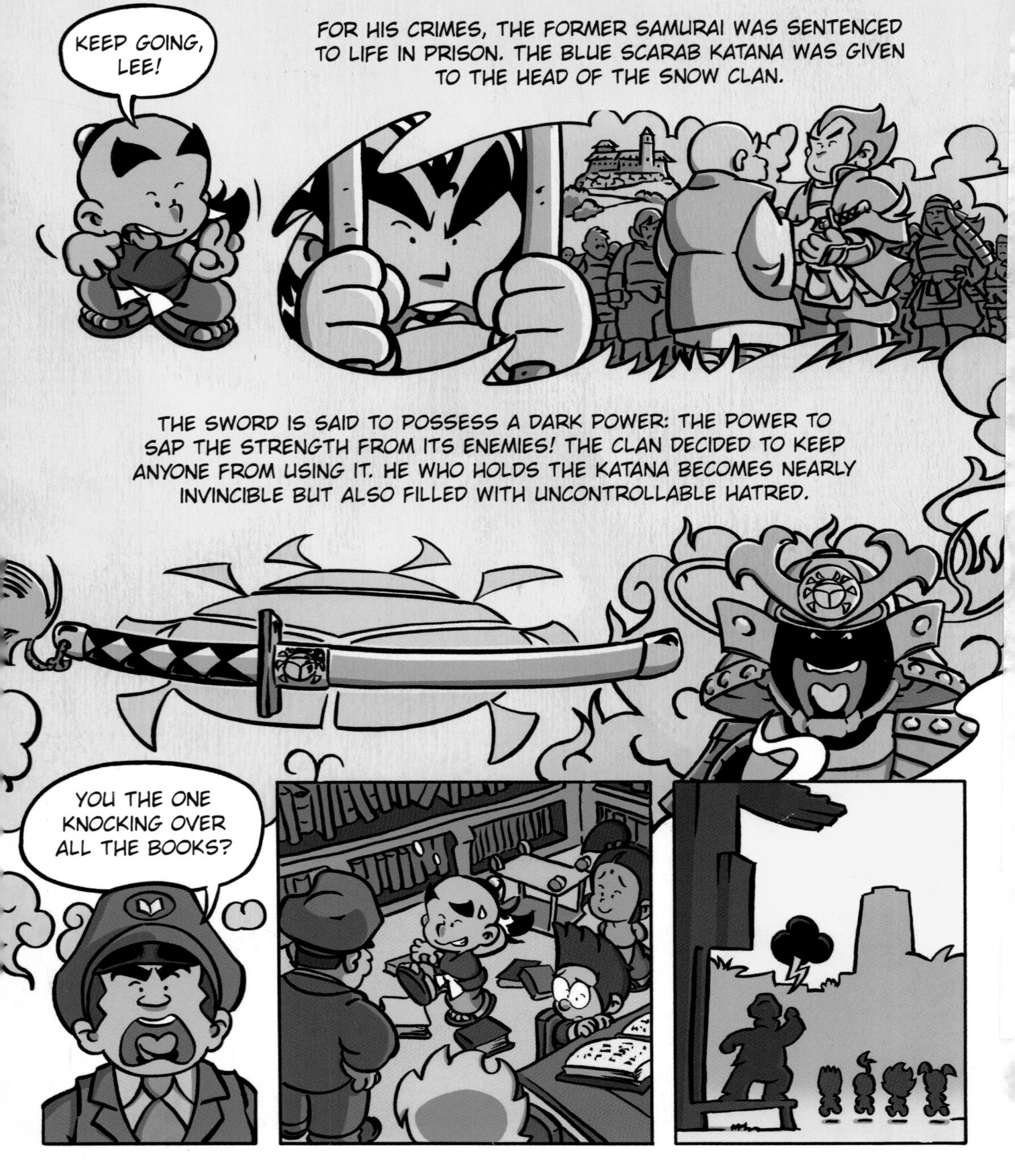
KEEP GOING, LEE!
FOR HIS CRIMES, THE FORMER SAMURAI WAS SENTENCED TO LIFE IN PRISON. THE BLUE SCARAB KATANA WAS GIVEN TO THE HEAD OF THE SNOW CLAN.
THE SWORD IS SAID TO POSSESS A DARK POWER: THE POWER TO SAP THE STRENGTH FROM ITS ENEMIES! THE CLAN DECIDED TO KEEP ANYONE FROM USING IT. HE WHO HOLDS THE KATANA BECOMES NEARLY INVINCIBLE BUT ALSO FILLED WITH UNCONTROLLABLE HATRED.
YOU THE ONE KNOCKING OVER ALL THE BOOKS?

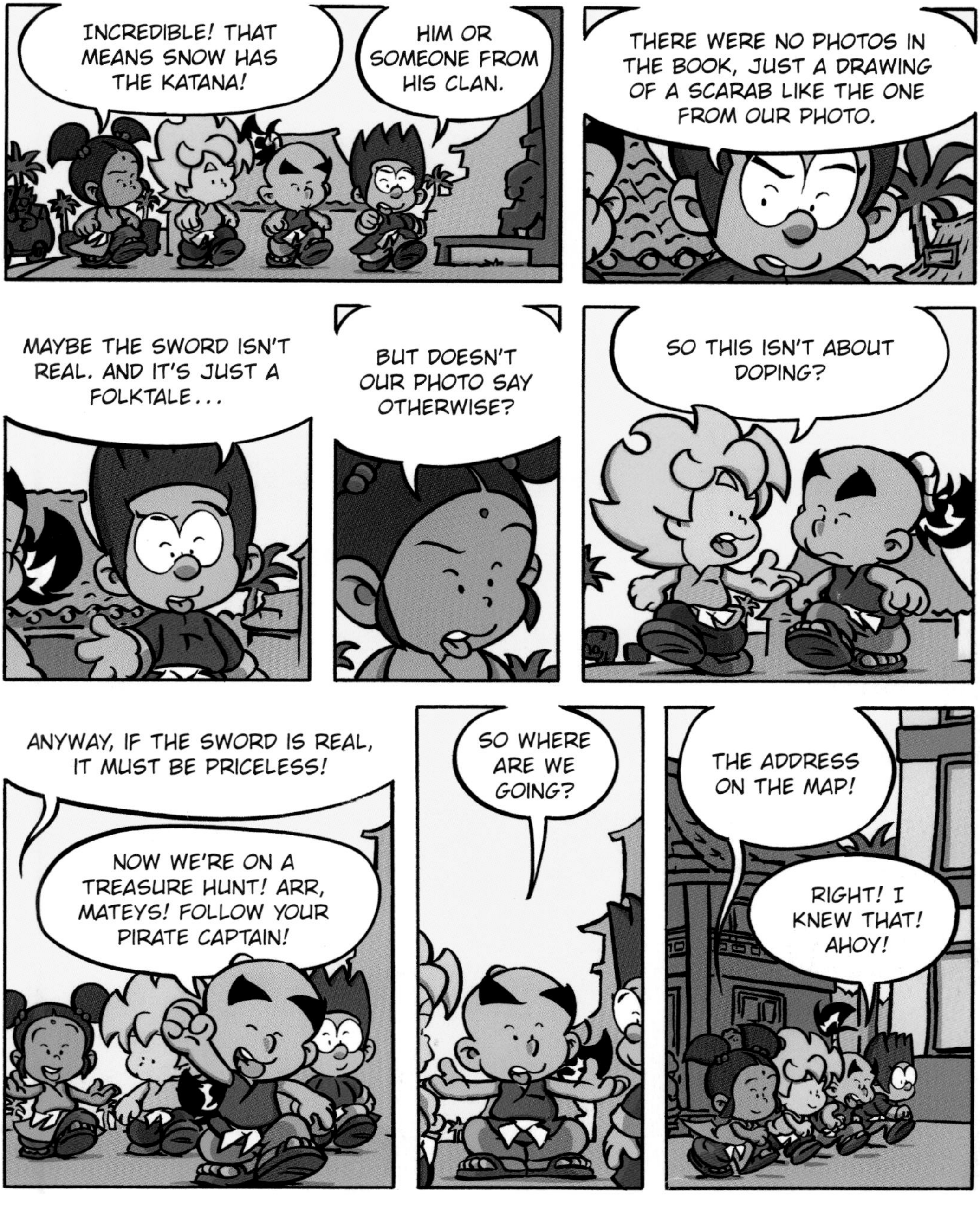
INCREDIBLE! THAT MEANS SNOW HAS THE KATANA!
HIM OR SOMEONE FROM HIS CLAN.
THERE WERE NO PHOTOS IN THE BOOK, JUST A DRAWING OF A SCARAB LIKE THE ONE FROM OUR PHOTO.
MAYBE THE SWORD ISN'T REAL. AND IT'S JUST A FOLKTALE...
BUT DOESN'T OUR PHOTO SAY OTHERWISE?
SO THIS ISN'T ABOUT DOPING?
ANYWAY, IF THE SWORD IS REAL, IT MUST BE PRICELESS!
NOW WE'RE ON A TREASURE HUNT! ARR, MATEYS! FOLLOW YOUR PIRATE CAPTAIN!
SO WHERE ARE WE GOING?
THE ADDRESS ON THE MAP!
RIGHT! I KNEW THAT! AHOY!

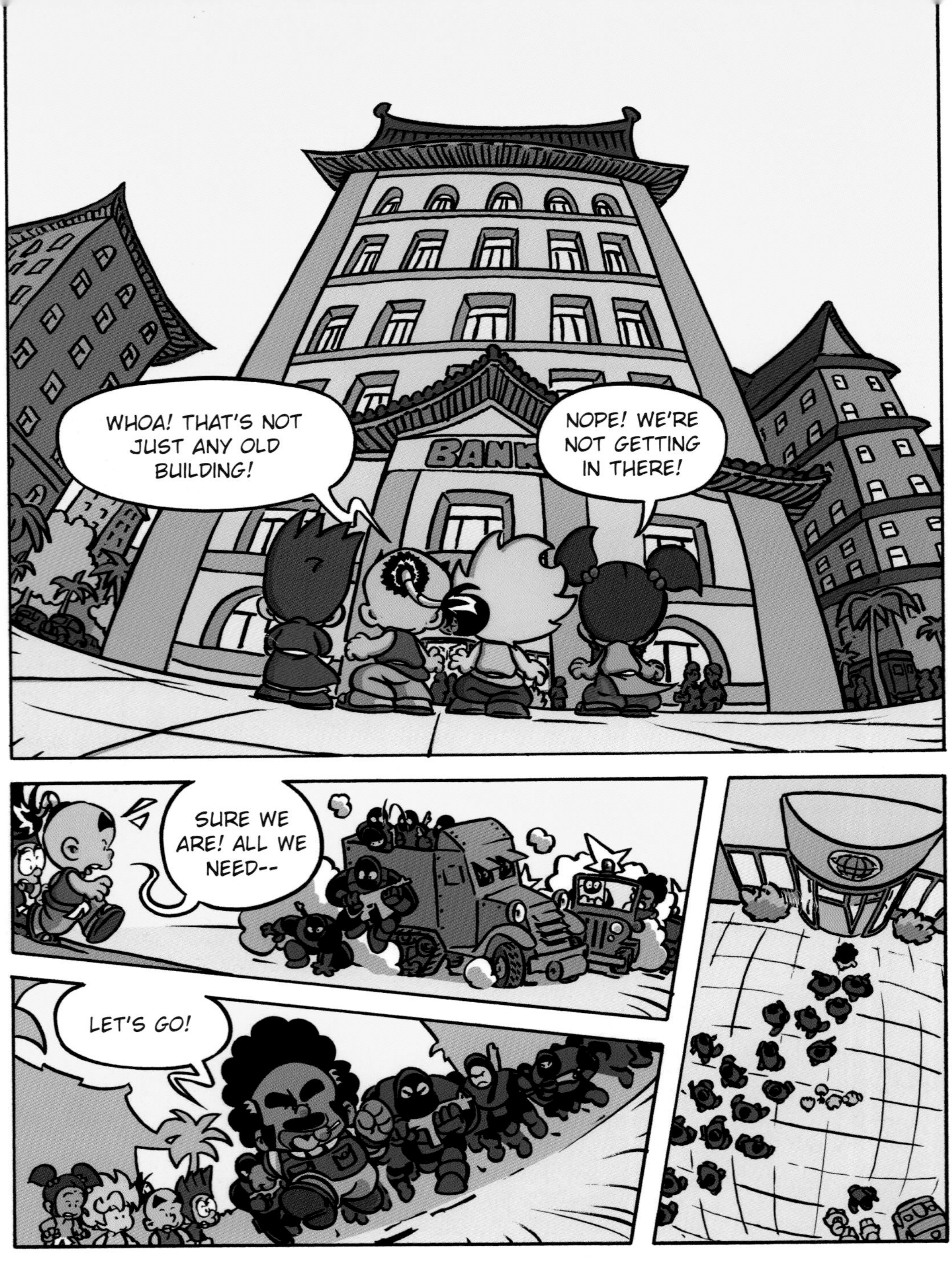
WHOA! THAT'S NOT JUST ANY OLD BUILDING!
NOPE! WE'RE NOT GETTING IN THERE!
BANK
SURE WE ARE! ALL WE NEED--
LET'S GO!

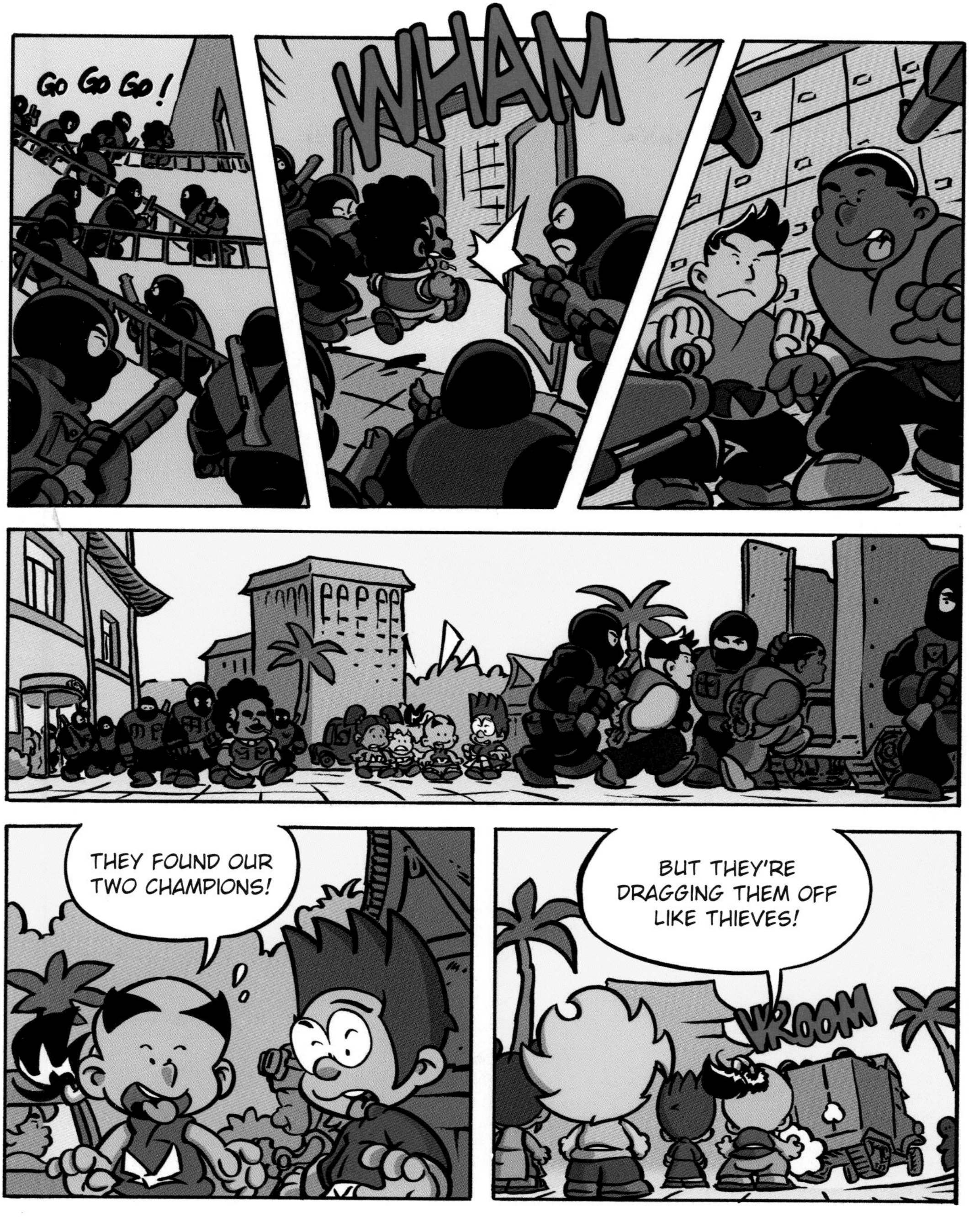
GO GO GO!
WHAM
THEY FOUND OUR TWO CHAMPIONS!
BUT THEY'RE DRAGGING THEM OFF LIKE THIEVES!
VROOM

28

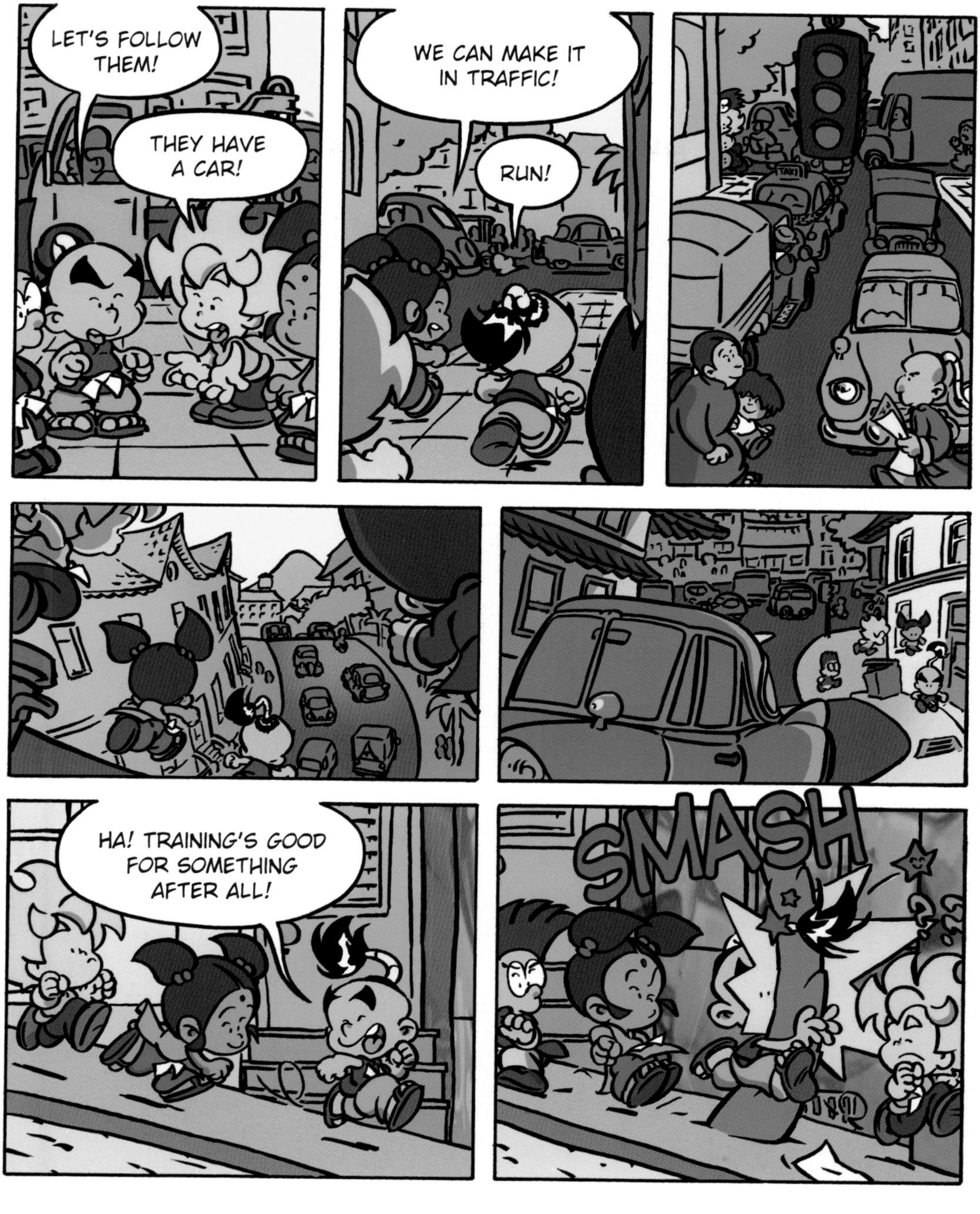
LET'S FOLLOW THEM!
THEY HAVE A CAR!
WE CAN MAKE IT IN TRAFFIC!
RUN!
HA! TRAINING'S GOOD FOR SOMETHING AFTER ALL!
SMASH

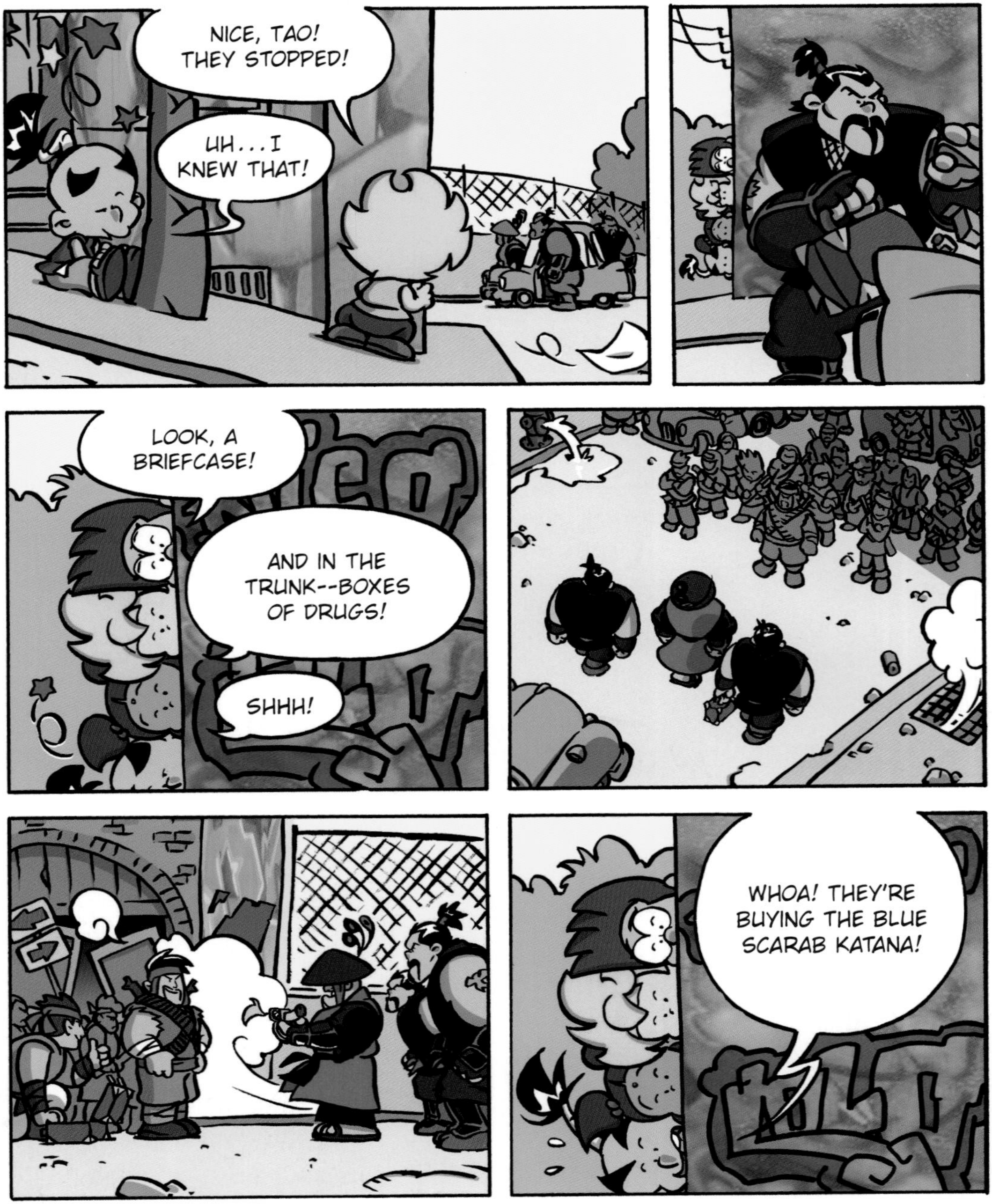
NICE, TAO! THEY STOPPED!
UH...I KNEW THAT!
LOOK, A BRIEFCASE!
AND IN THE TRUNK--BOXES OF DRUGS!
SHHH!
WHOA! THEY'RE BUYING THE BLUE SCARAB KATANA!

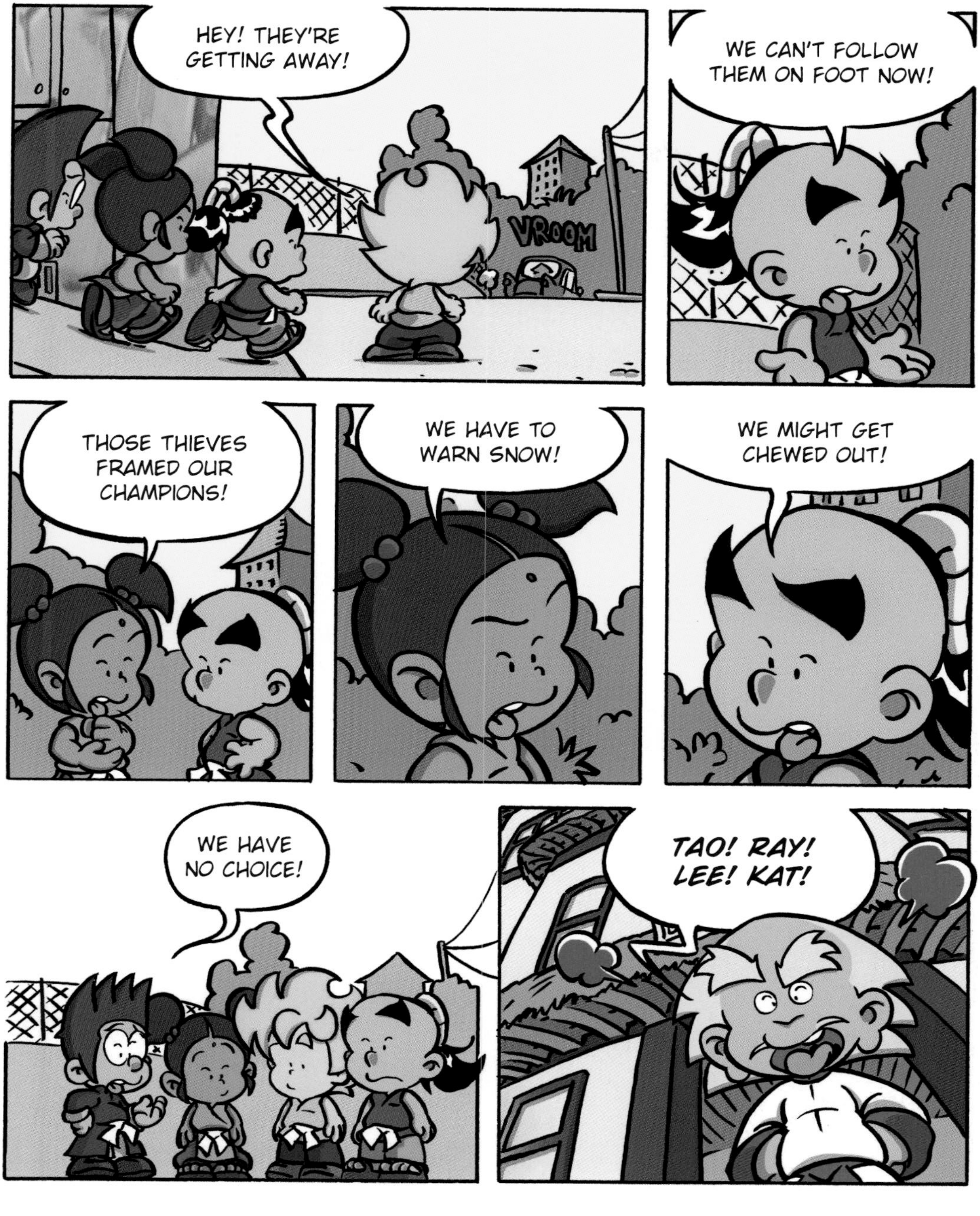
HEY! THEY'RE GETTING AWAY!
VROOM
WE CAN'T FOLLOW THEM ON FOOT NOW!
THOSE THIEVES FRAMED OUR CHAMPIONS!
WE HAVE TO WARN SNOW!
WE MIGHT GET CHEWED OUT!
WE HAVE NO CHOICE!
TAO! RAY! LEE! KAT!

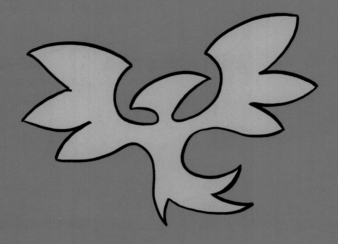

The phoenix Clan

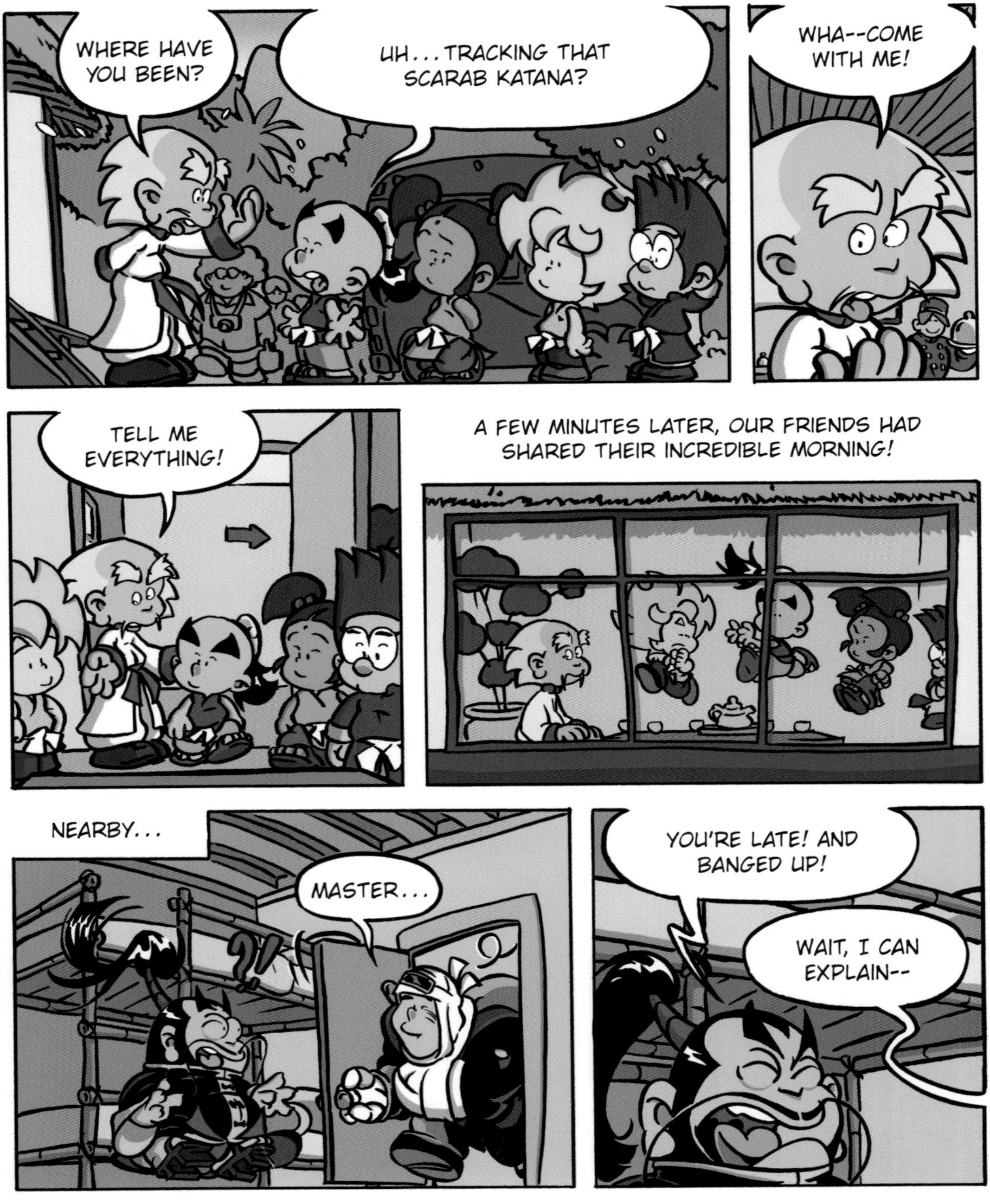
WHERE HAVE YOU BEEN?
UH... TRACKING THAT SCARAB KATANA?
WHA--COME WITH ME!
TELL ME EVERYTHING!
A FEW MINUTES LATER, OUR FRIENDS HAD SHARED THEIR INCREDIBLE MORNING!
NEARBY...
MASTER...
?!
YOU'RE LATE! AND BANGED UP!
WAIT, I CAN EXPLAIN--

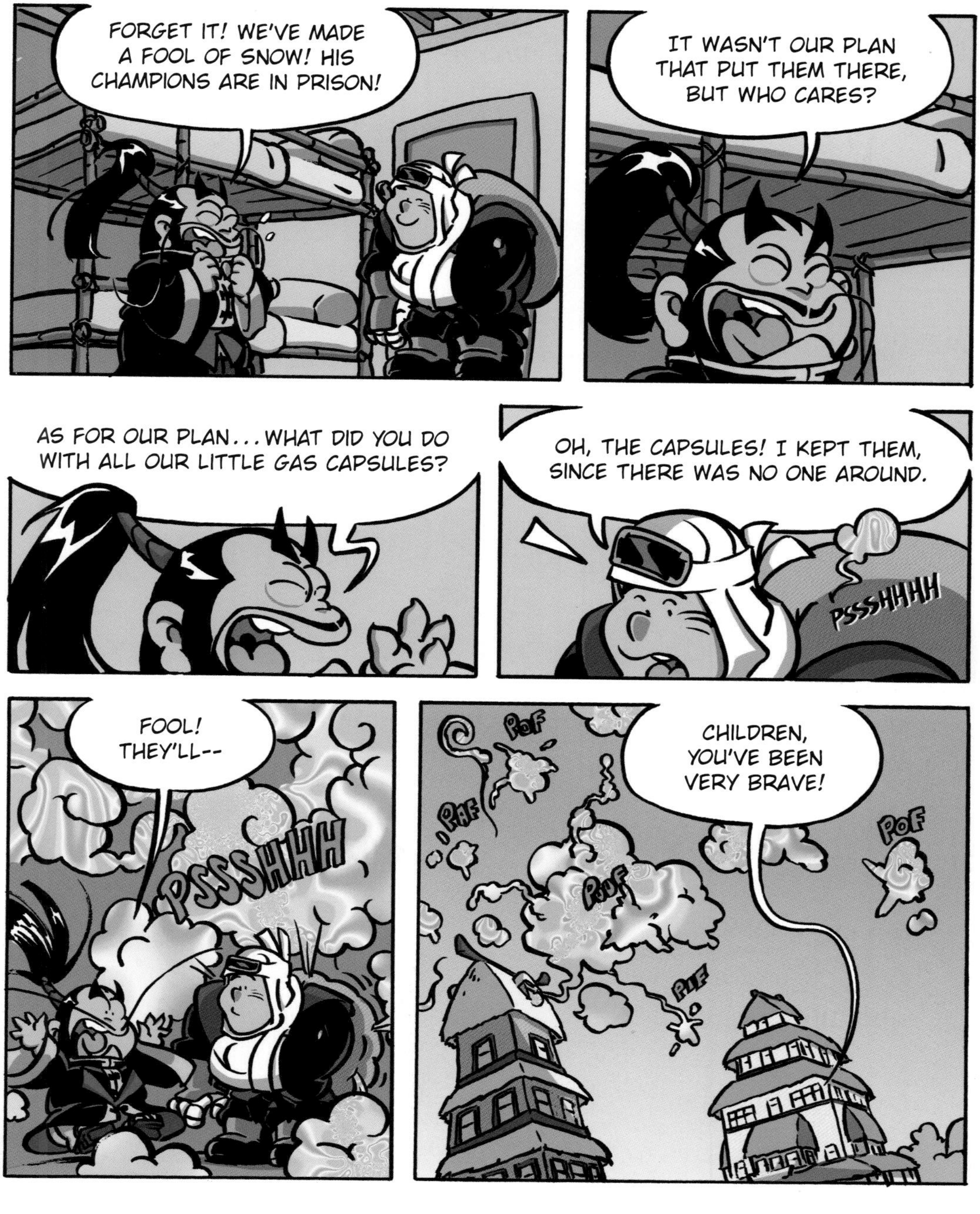

FORGET IT! WE'VE MADE A FOOL OF SNOW! HIS CHAMPIONS ARE IN PRISON!
IT WASN'T OUR PLAN THAT PUT THEM THERE, BUT WHO CARES?
AS FOR OUR PLAN... WHAT DID YOU DO WITH ALL OUR LITTLE GAS CAPSULES?
OH, THE CAPSULES! I KEPT THEM, SINCE THERE WAS NO ONE AROUND.
PSSSHHHH
FOOL! THEY'LL--
PSSSHHHH
POF
PAF
POF
PUF
PUF
CHILDREN, YOU'VE BEEN VERY BRAVE!

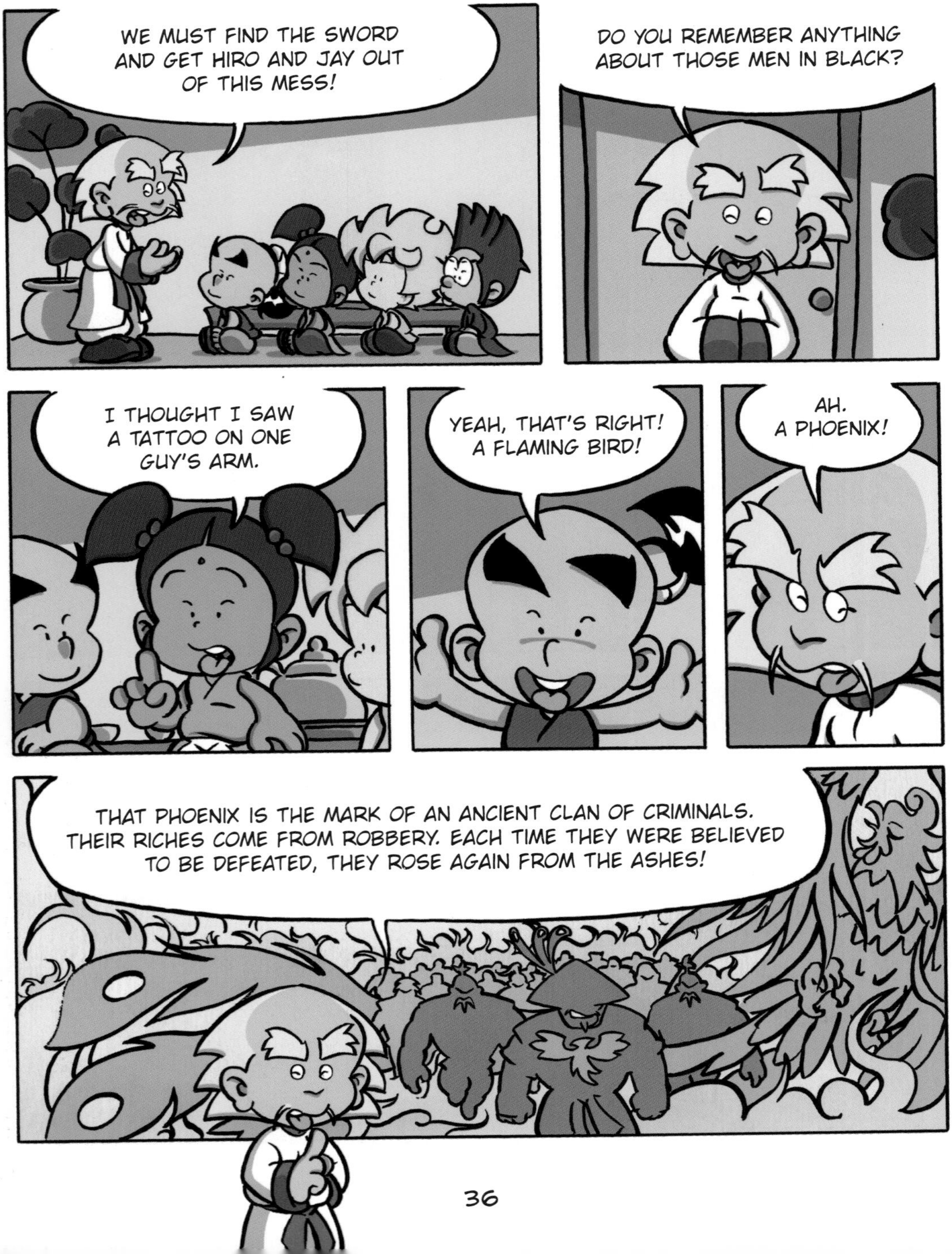
WE MUST FIND THE SWORD AND GET HIRO AND JAY OUT OF THIS MESS!
DO YOU REMEMBER ANYTHING ABOUT THOSE MEN IN BLACK?
I THOUGHT I SAW A TATTOO ON ONE GUY'S ARM.
YEAH, THAT'S RIGHT! A FLAMING BIRD!
AH. A PHOENIX!
THAT PHOENIX IS THE MARK OF AN ANCIENT CLAN OF CRIMINALS. THEIR RICHES COME FROM ROBBERY. EACH TIME THEY WERE BELIEVED TO BE DEFEATED, THEY ROSE AGAIN FROM THE ASHES!

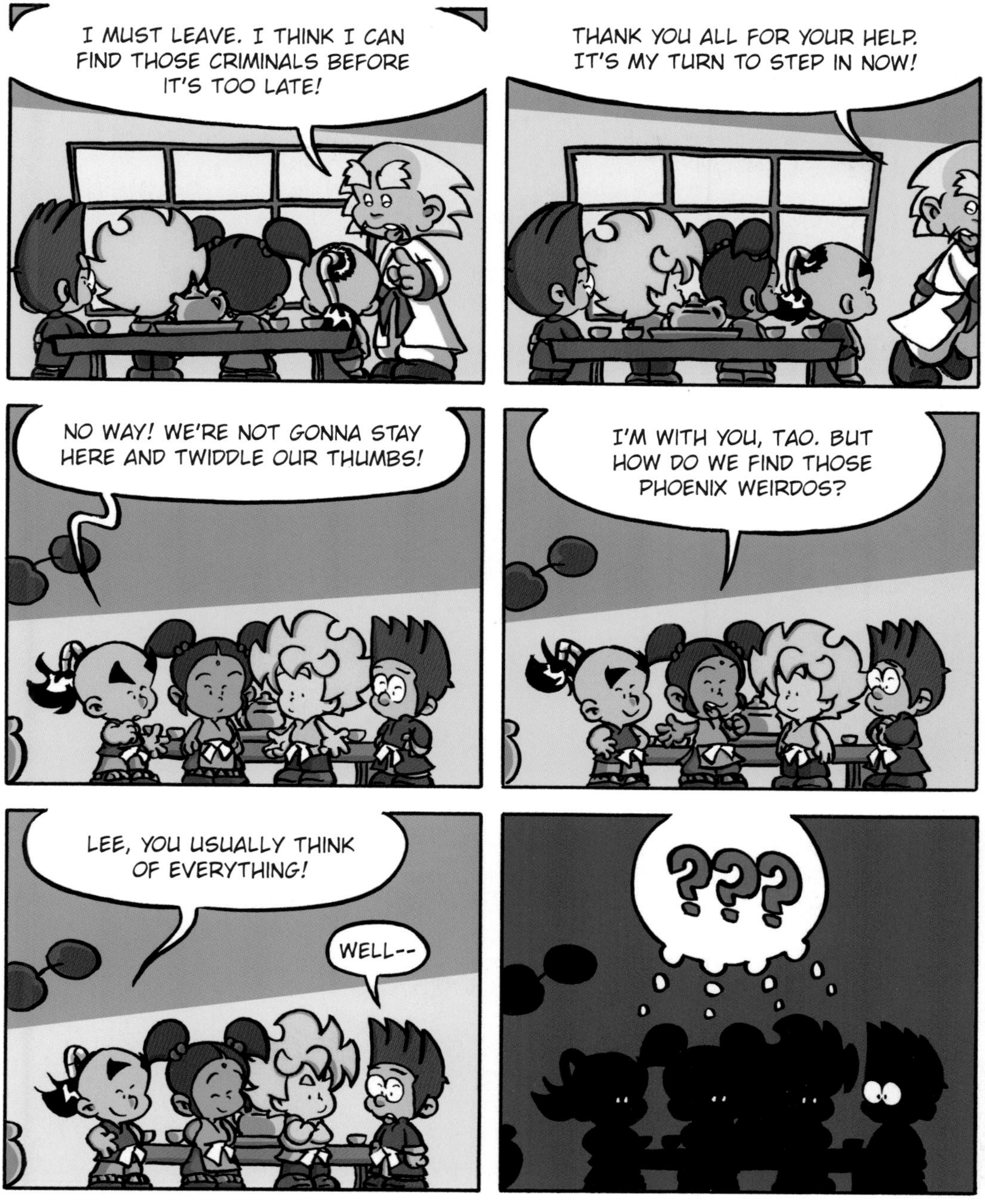
I MUST LEAVE. I THINK I CAN FIND THOSE CRIMINALS BEFORE IT'S TOO LATE!
THANK YOU ALL FOR YOUR HELP. IT'S MY TURN TO STEP IN NOW!
NO WAY! WE'RE NOT GONNA STAY HERE AND TWIDDLE OUR THUMBS!
I'M WITH YOU, TAO. BUT HOW DO WE FIND THOSE PHOENIX WEIRDOS?
LEE, YOU USUALLY THINK OF EVERYTHING!
WELL--
???

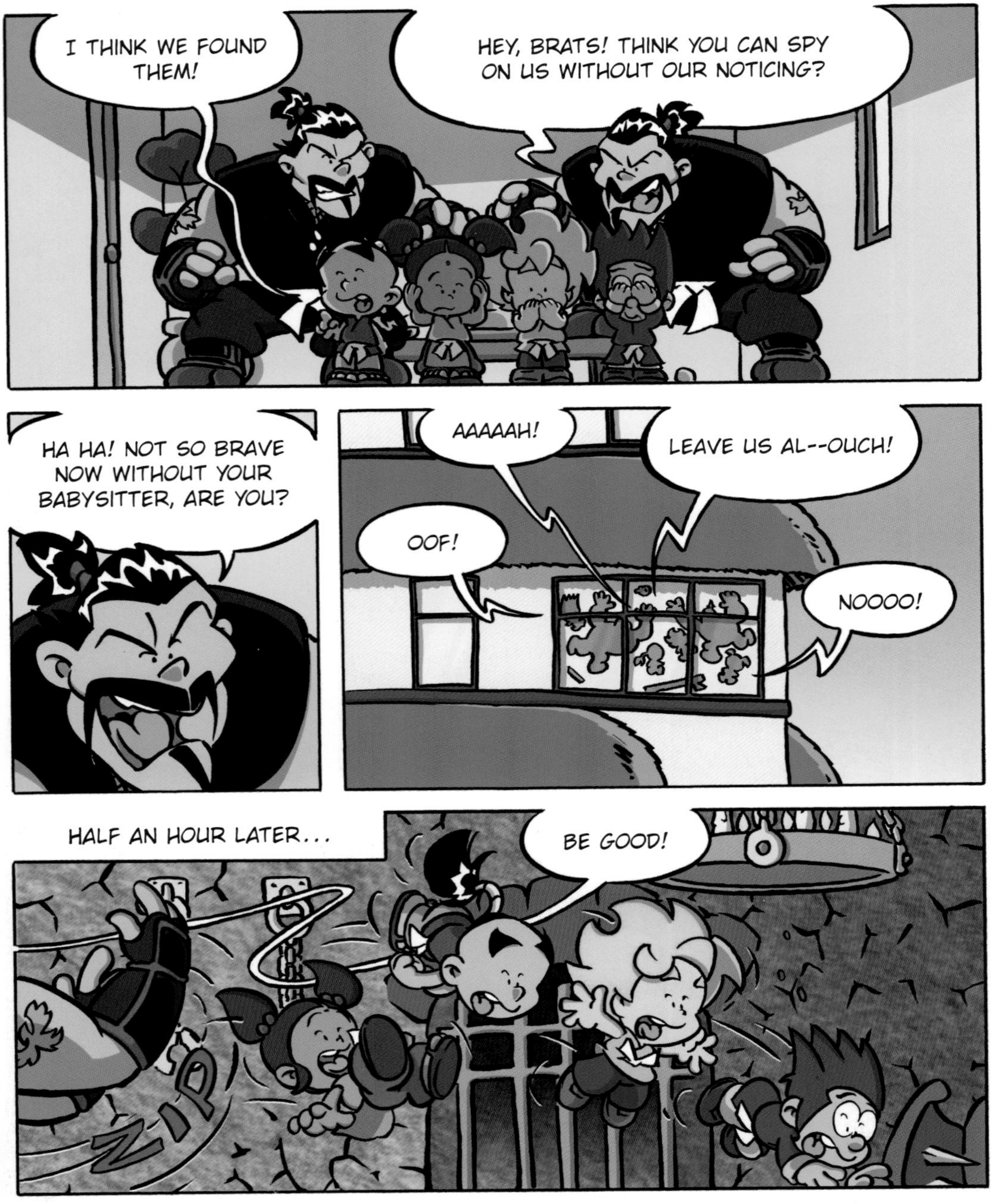
I THINK WE FOUND THEM!
HEY, BRATS! THINK YOU CAN SPY ON US WITHOUT OUR NOTICING?
HA HA! NOT SO BRAVE NOW WITHOUT YOUR BABYSITTER, ARE YOU?
AAAAAH!
LEAVE US AL--OUCH!
OOF!
NOOOO!
HALF AN HOUR LATER...
BE GOOD!
ZIP

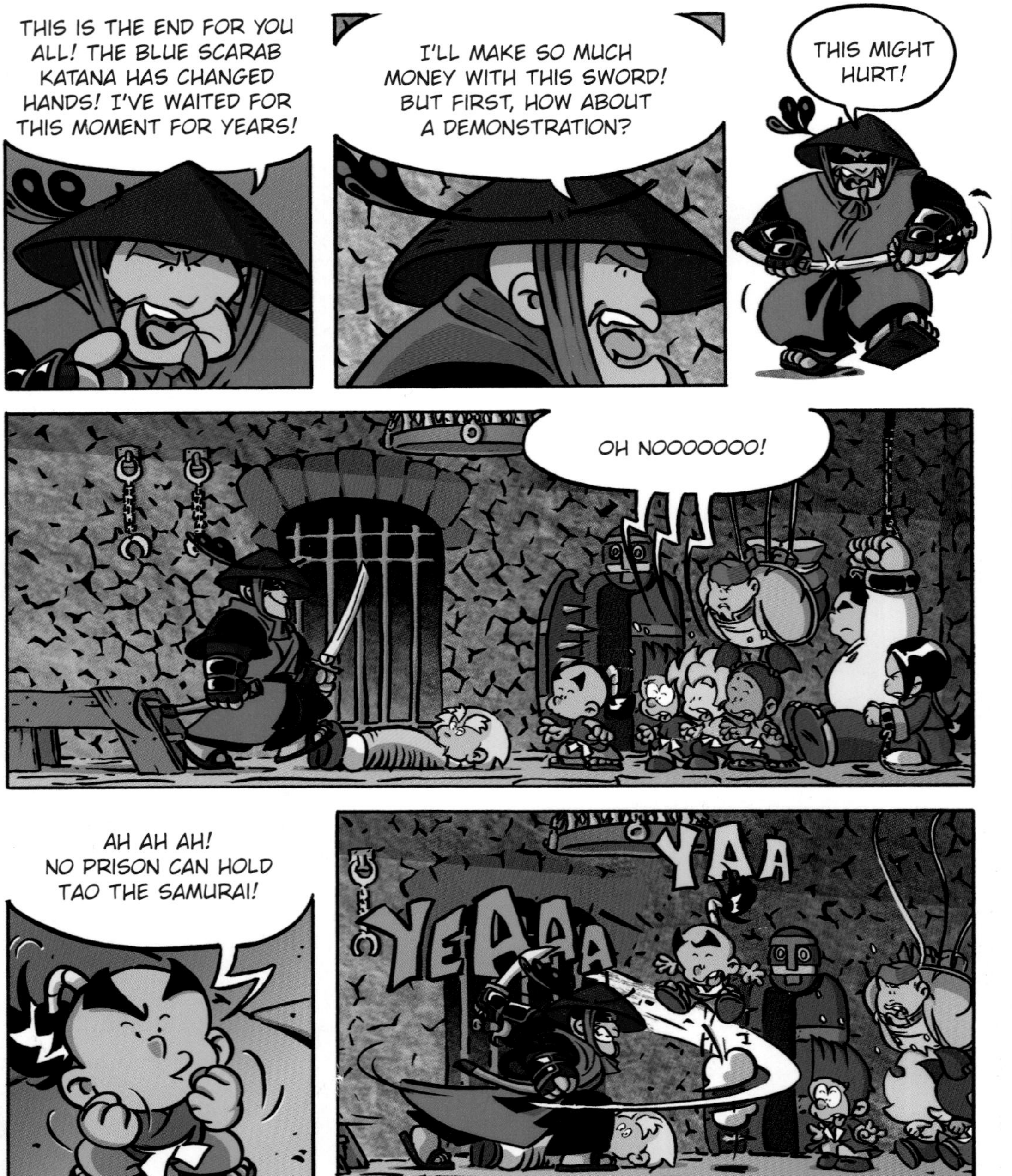
THIS IS THE END FOR YOU ALL! THE BLUE SCARAB KATANA HAS CHANGED HANDS! I'VE WAITED FOR THIS MOMENT FOR YEARS!
I'LL MAKE SO MUCH MONEY WITH THIS SWORD! BUT FIRST, HOW ABOUT A DEMONSTRATION?
THIS MIGHT HURT!
OH NOOOOOOO!
AH AH AH! NO PRISON CAN HOLD TAO THE SAMURAI!
YEAAA
YAA

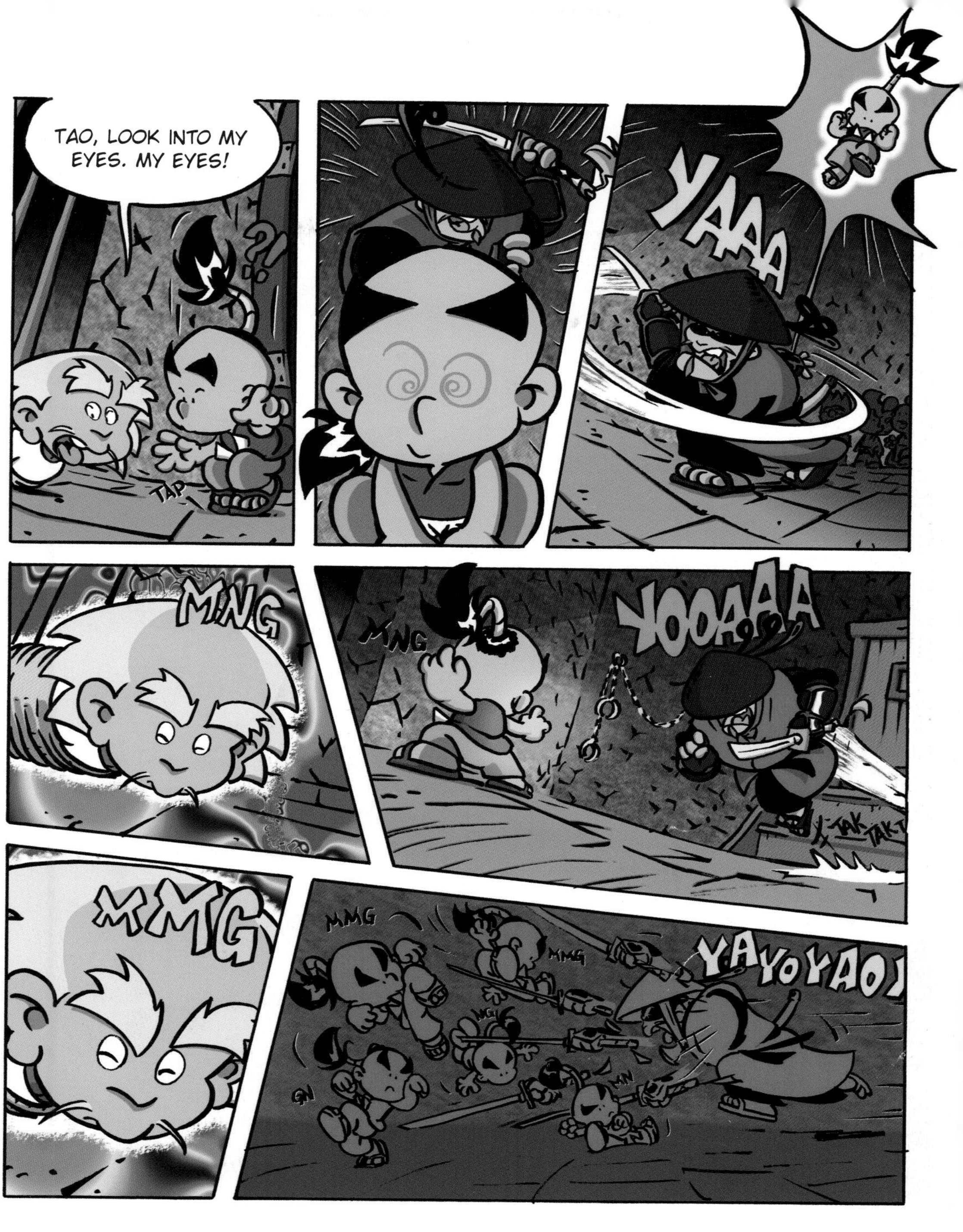

TAO, LOOK INTO MY EYES. MY EYES!
?!
TAP
YAAA
MNG
MNG
YOOAAAA
TAK TAK
MMG
MMG
MMG
YAYOYAO
GN

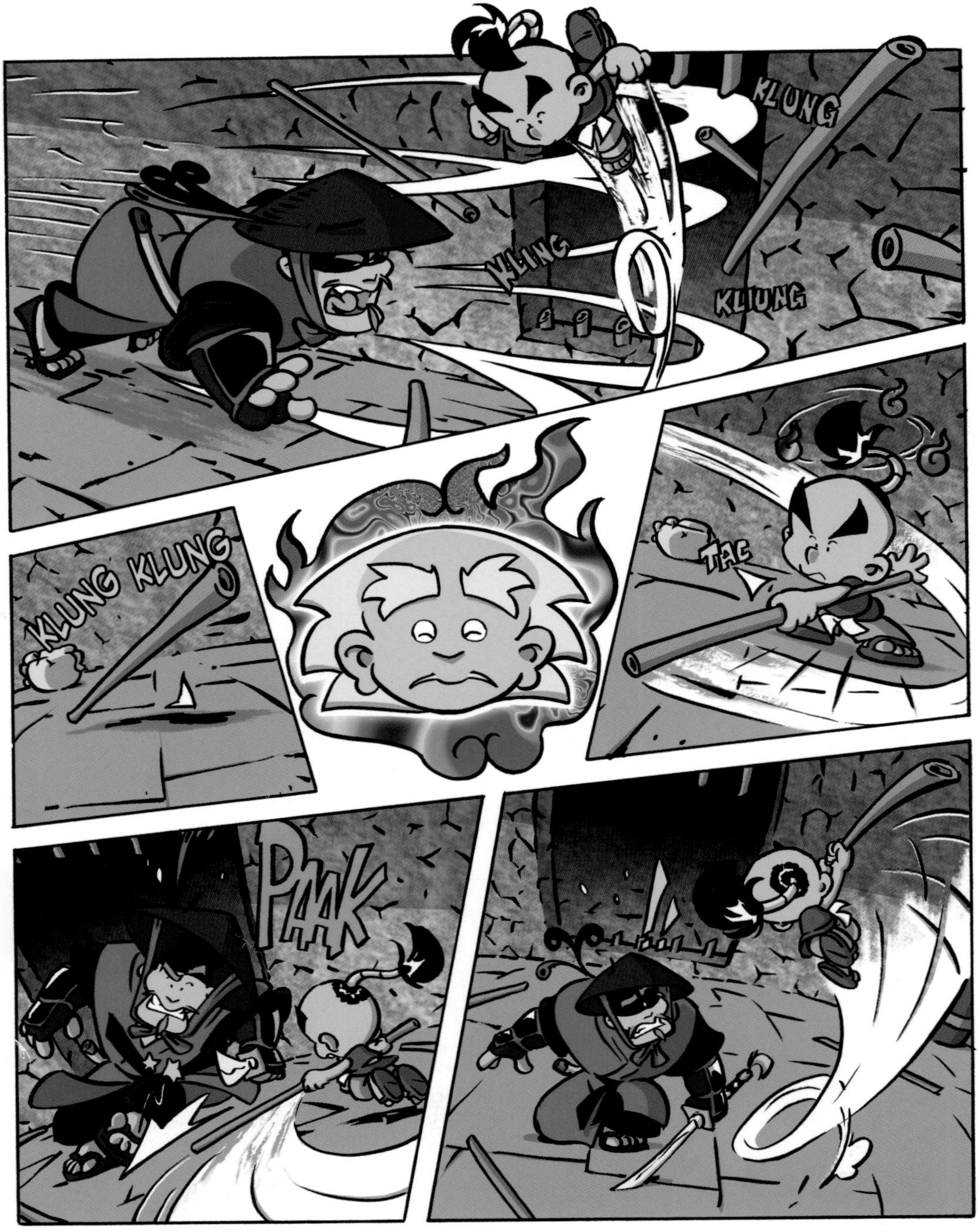
KLUNG
KLING
KLIUNG
KLUNG KLUNG
TAC
PAAK

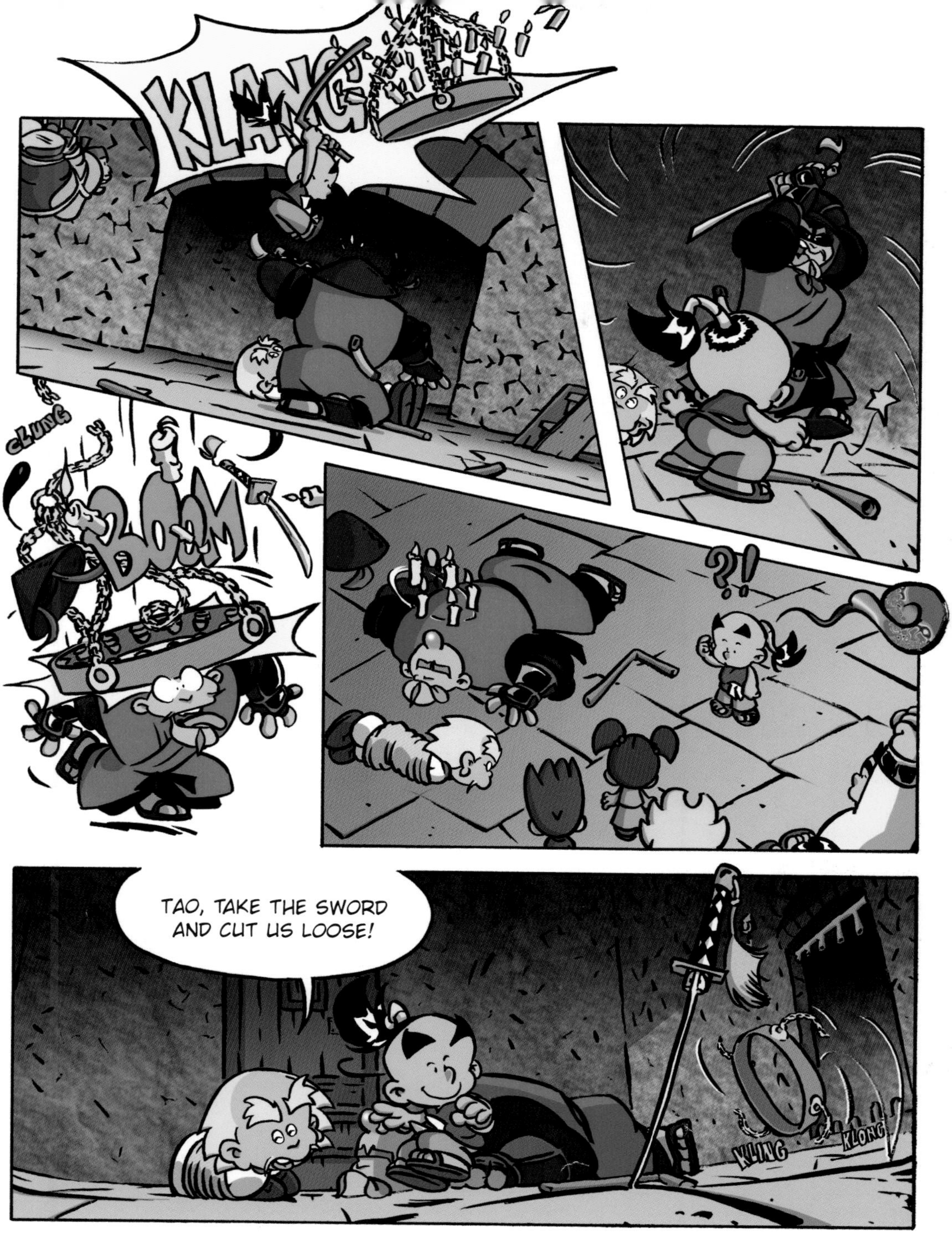
KLANG
CLUNG
BOOM
?!
TAO, TAKE THE SWORD AND CUT US LOOSE!
KLING
KLONG

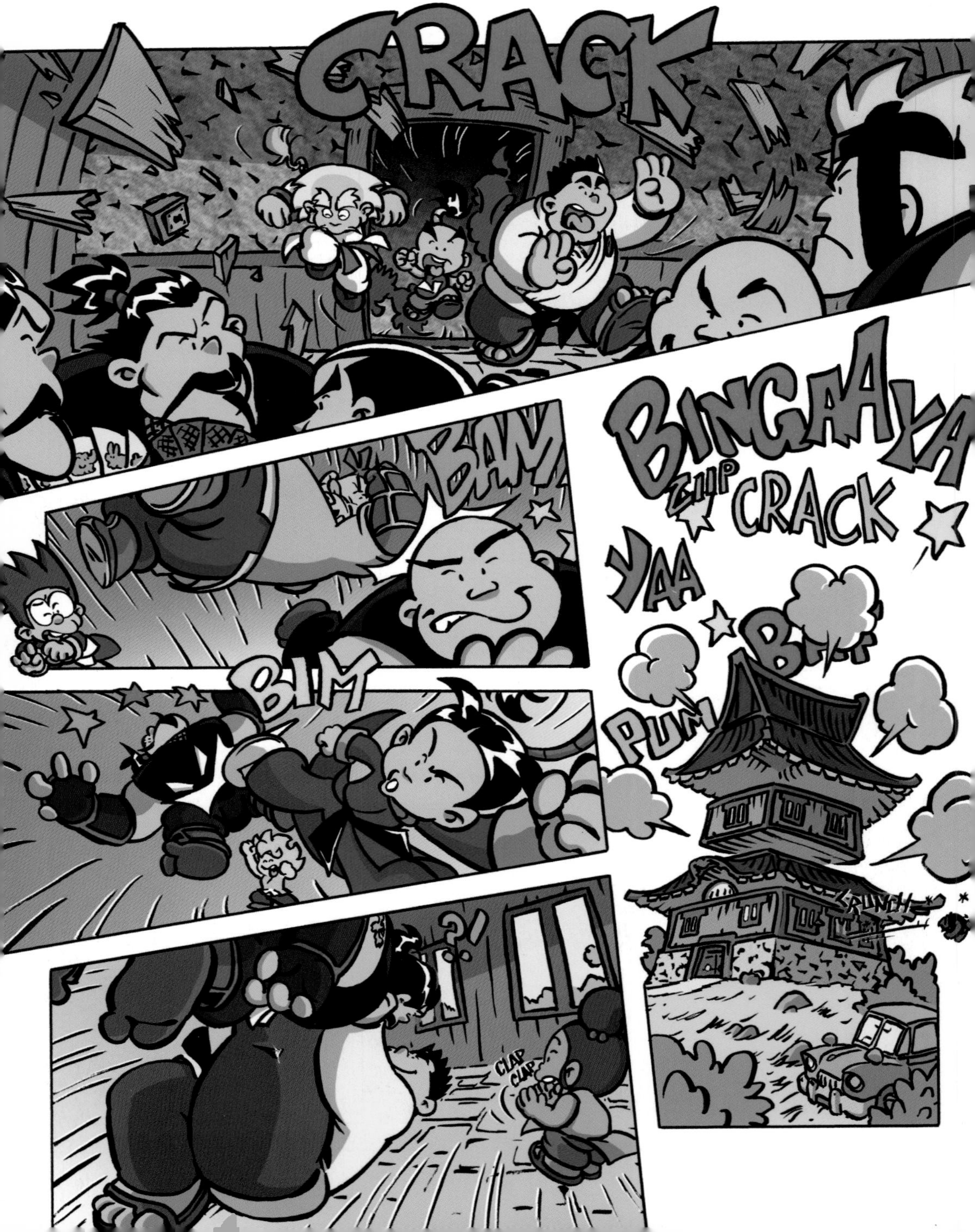
CRACK
BAM
BINGAAYA
ZIIP
CRACK
YAA
BIM
PUM
CRUNCH
?!
CLAP CLAP

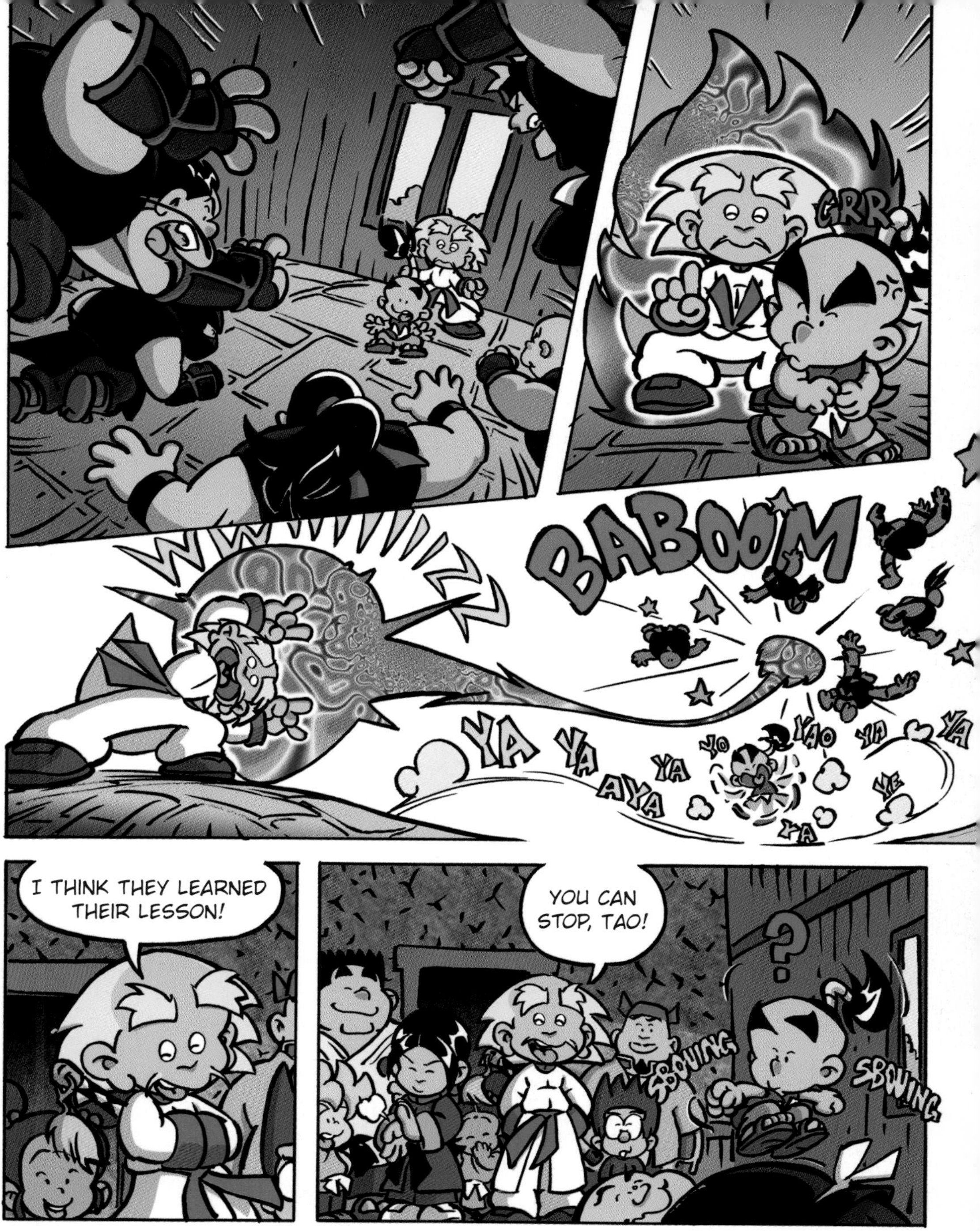
GRR
BABOOM
YA YA AYA YA YO YAO YA YA YE YA
I THINK THEY LEARNED THEIR LESSON!
YOU CAN STOP, TAO!
?
SBOING
SBOING

The Final Chapter

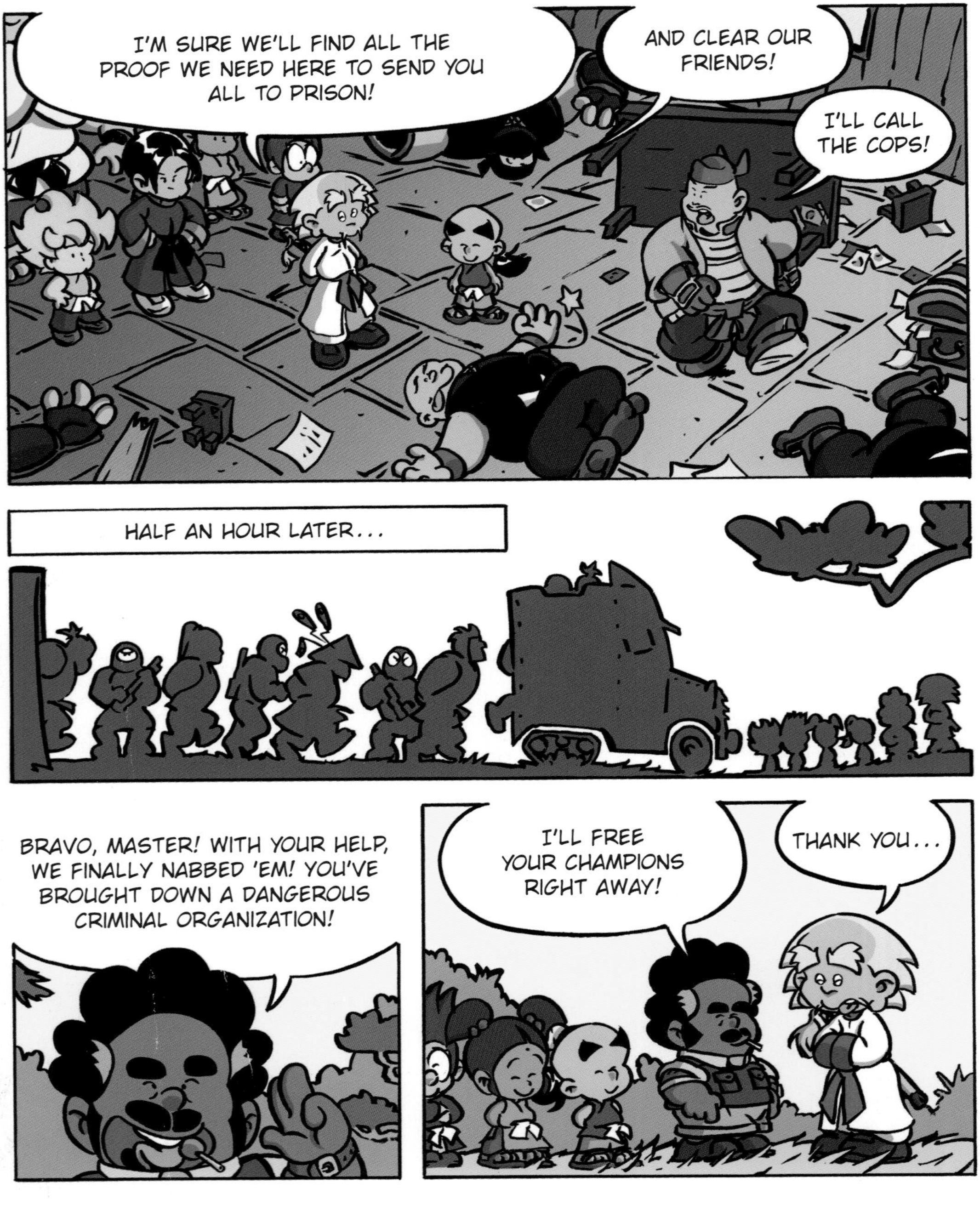
I'M SURE WE'LL FIND ALL THE PROOF WE NEED HERE TO SEND YOU ALL TO PRISON!
AND CLEAR OUR FRIENDS!
I'LL CALL THE COPS!
HALF AN HOUR LATER...
BRAVO, MASTER! WITH YOUR HELP, WE FINALLY NABBED 'EM! YOU'VE BROUGHT DOWN A DANGEROUS CRIMINAL ORGANIZATION!
I'LL FREE YOUR CHAMPIONS RIGHT AWAY!
THANK YOU...

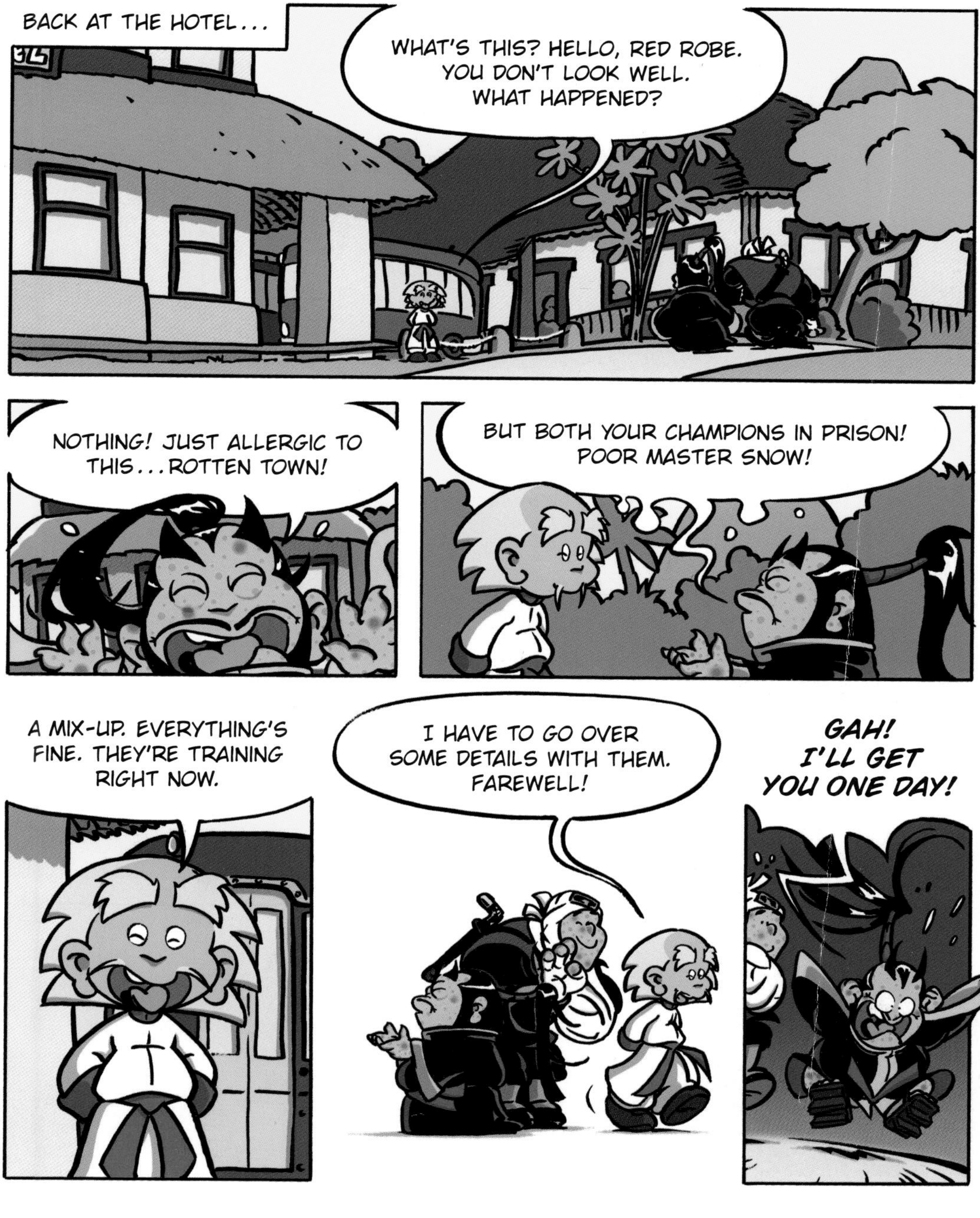
BACK AT THE HOTEL...
WHAT'S THIS? HELLO, RED ROBE. YOU DON'T LOOK WELL. WHAT HAPPENED?
NOTHING! JUST ALLERGIC TO THIS...ROTTEN TOWN!
BUT BOTH YOUR CHAMPIONS IN PRISON! POOR MASTER SNOW!
A MIX-UP. EVERYTHING'S FINE. THEY'RE TRAINING RIGHT NOW.
I HAVE TO GO OVER SOME DETAILS WITH THEM. FAREWELL!
GAH! I'LL GET YOU ONE DAY!

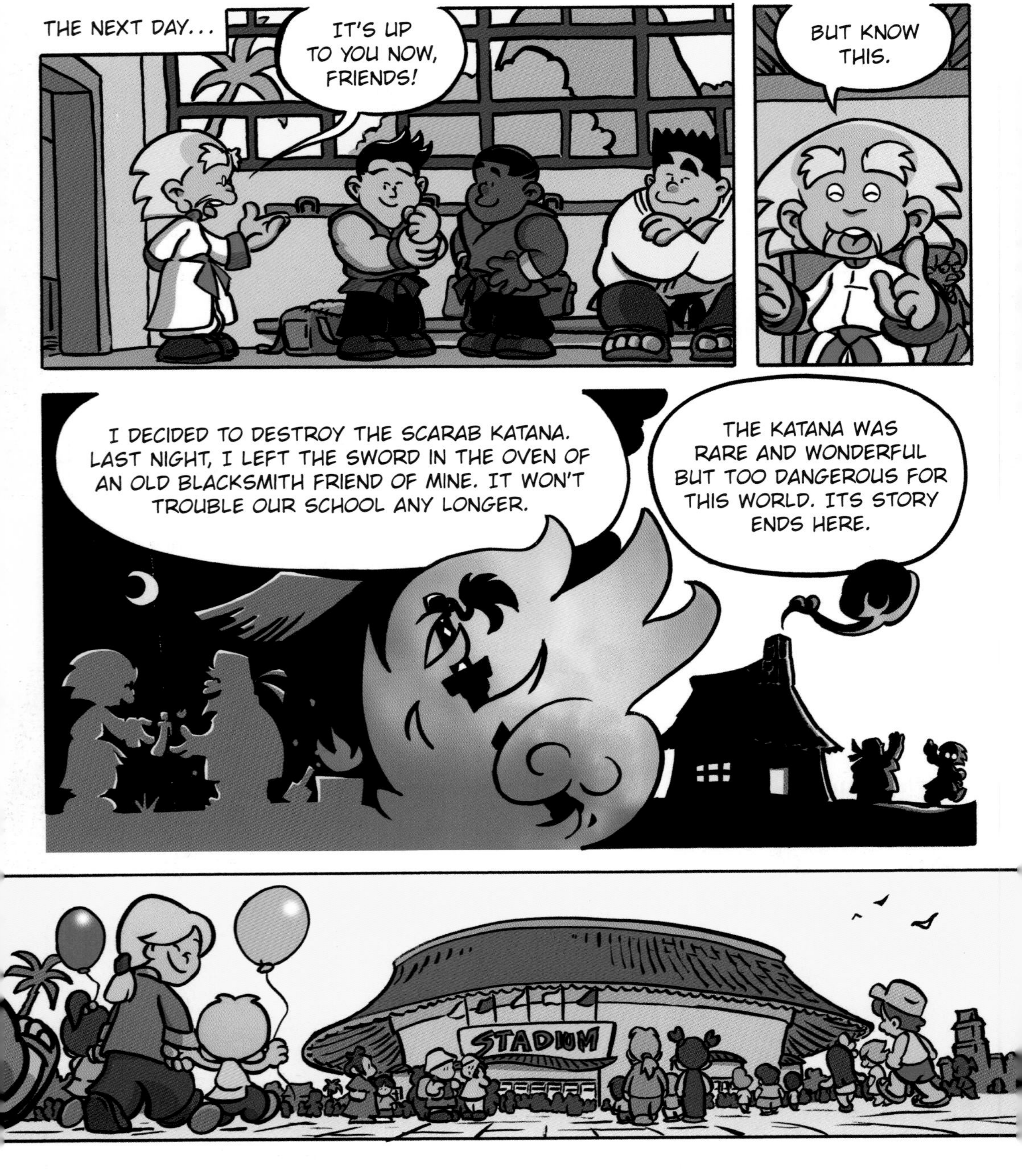
THE NEXT DAY...
IT'S UP TO YOU NOW, FRIENDS!
BUT KNOW THIS.
I DECIDED TO DESTROY THE SCARAB KATANA. LAST NIGHT, I LEFT THE SWORD IN THE OVEN OF AN OLD BLACKSMITH FRIEND OF MINE. IT WON'T TROUBLE OUR SCHOOL ANY LONGER.
THE KATANA WAS RARE AND WONDERFUL BUT TOO DANGEROUS FOR THIS WORLD. ITS STORY ENDS HERE.
STADIUM

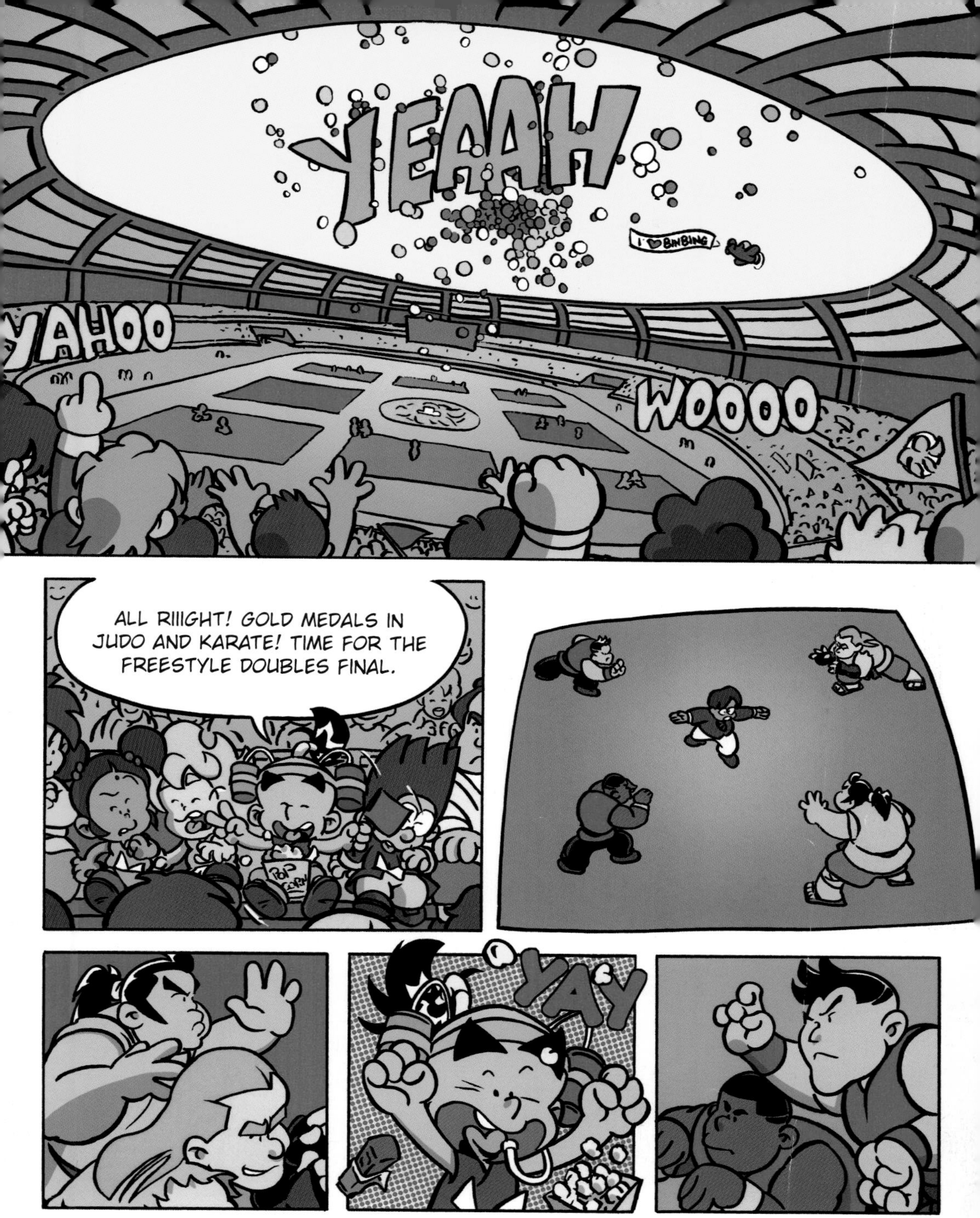
YEAAH
I ♥ BINBING
YAHOO
WOOOO
ALL RIIIGHT! GOLD MEDALS IN JUDO AND KARATE! TIME FOR THE FREESTYLE DOUBLES FINAL.
POP CORN
YAY

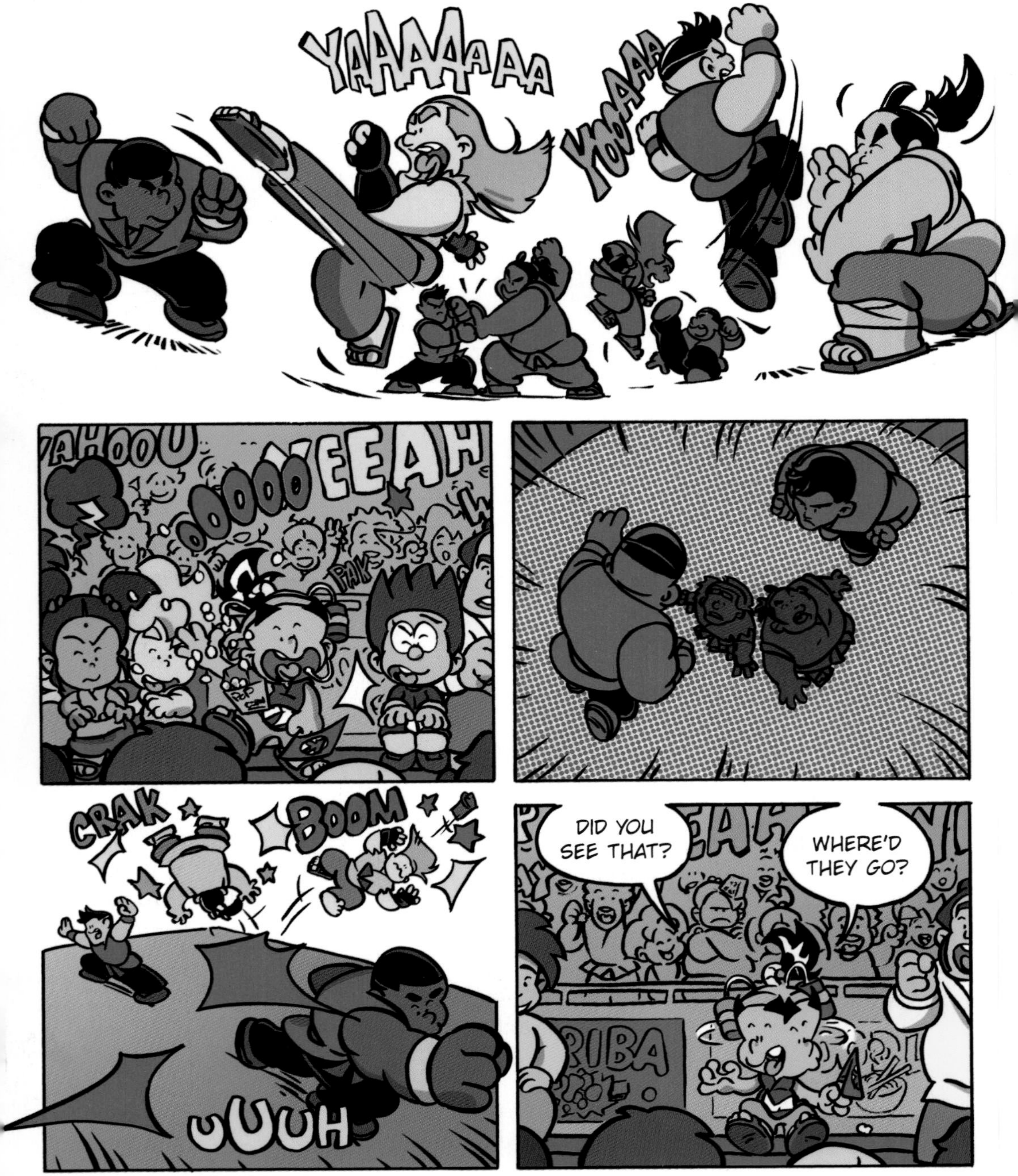
YAAAAAAA
YOOOAAA
AHOOU
OOOOO EEAH
PAK
CRAK
BOOM
UUUH
DID YOU SEE THAT?
WHERE'D THEY GO?
RIBA

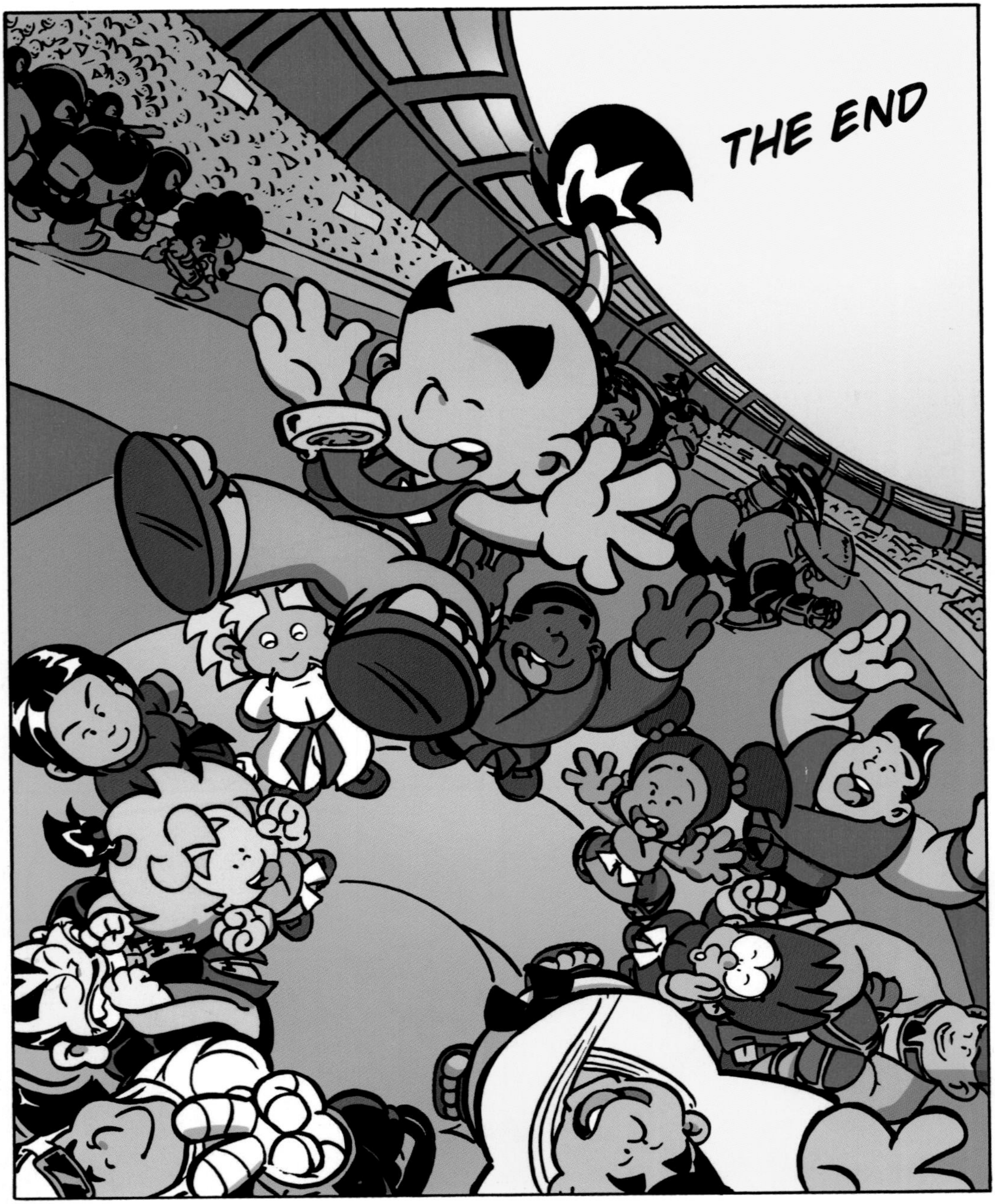
THE END

The Creators of Tao Present Their Desks!

WHAT A MESS!

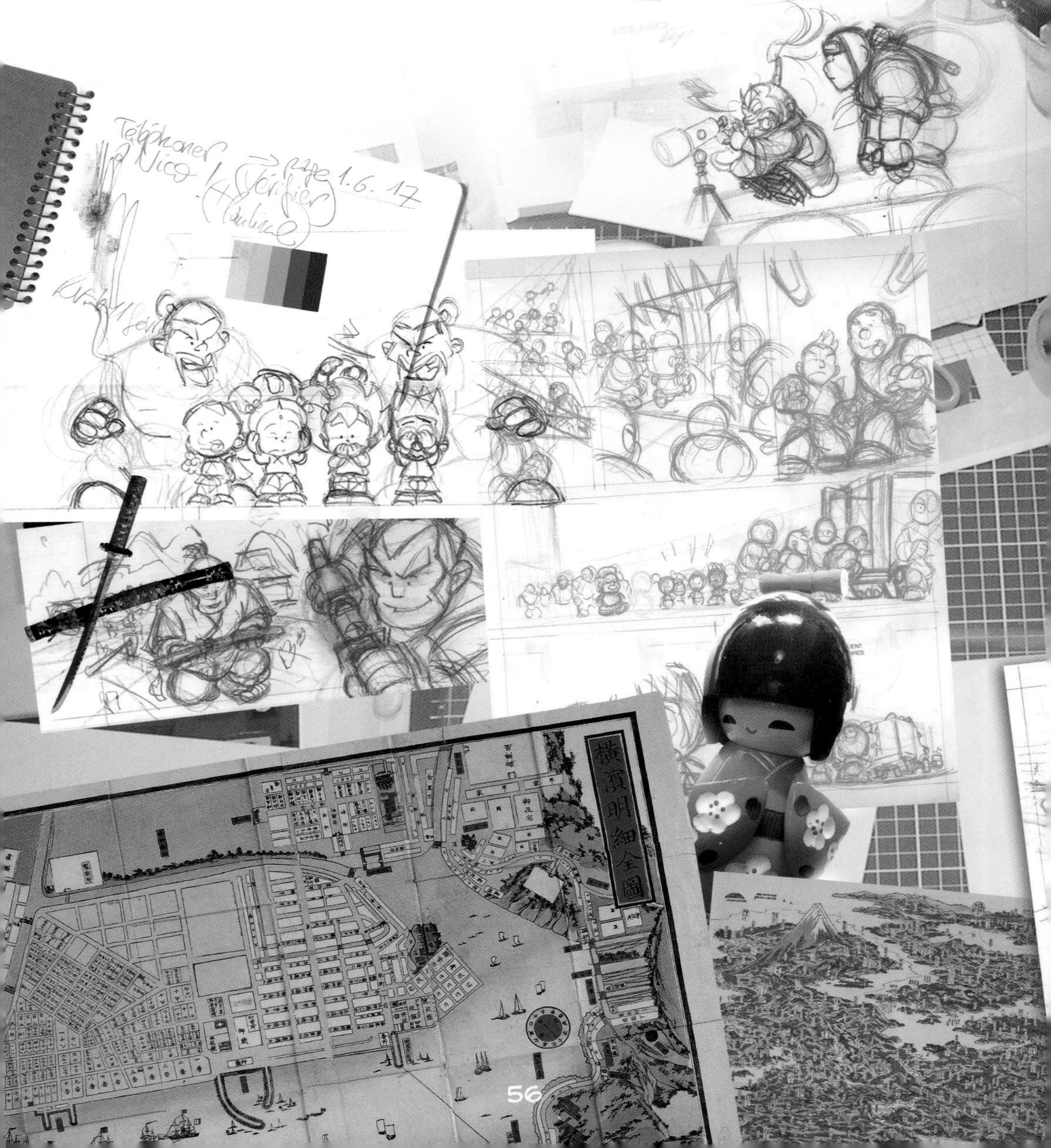
Téléphoner à Nico!
→ page 1.6.17
Vérifier (Pauline)
横濱明細全圖

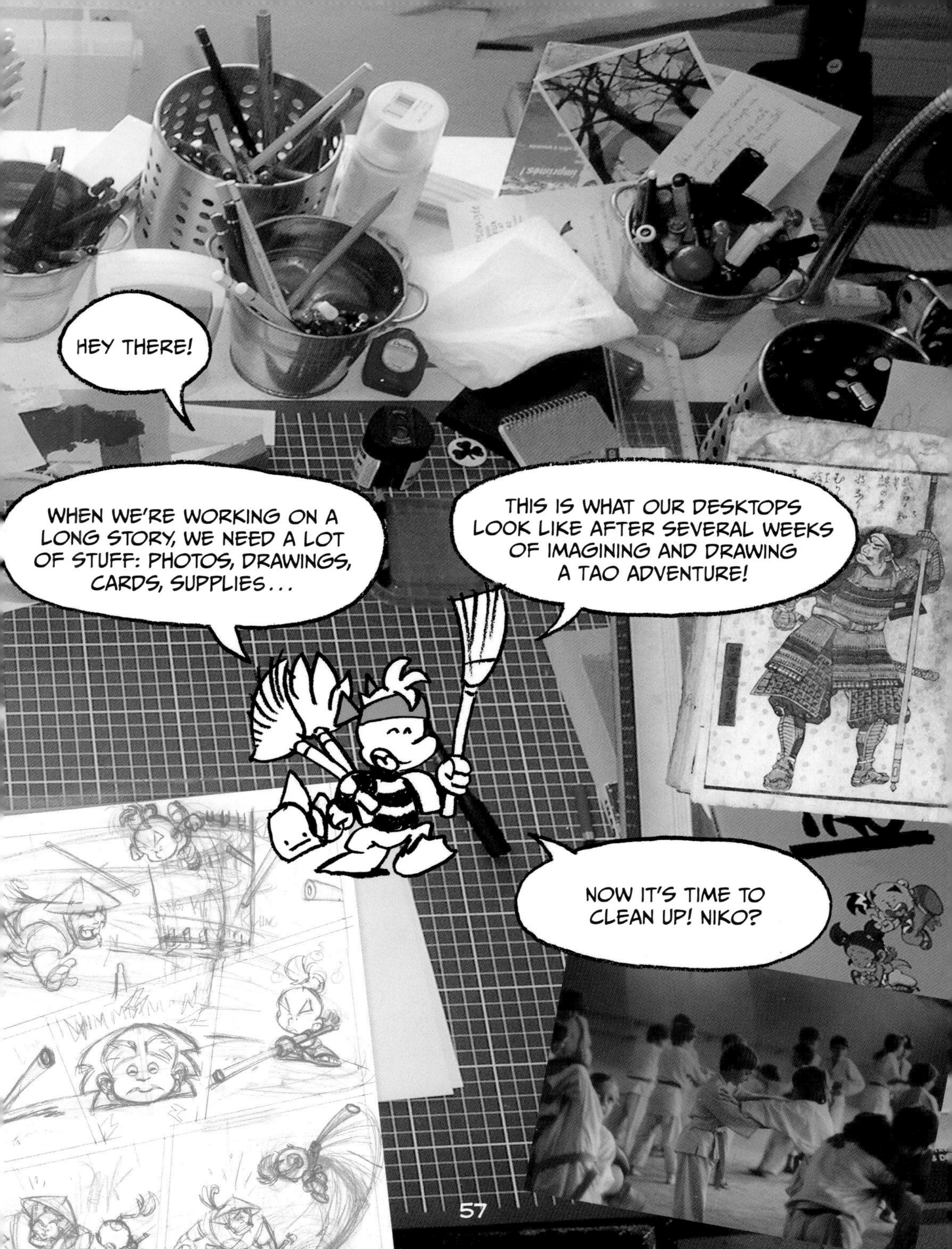
HEY THERE!
WHEN WE'RE WORKING ON A LONG STORY, WE NEED A LOT OF STUFF: PHOTOS, DRAWINGS, CARDS, SUPPLIES...
THIS IS WHAT OUR DESKTOPS LOOK LIKE AFTER SEVERAL WEEKS OF IMAGINING AND DRAWING A TAO ADVENTURE!
NOW IT'S TIME TO CLEAN UP! NIKO?

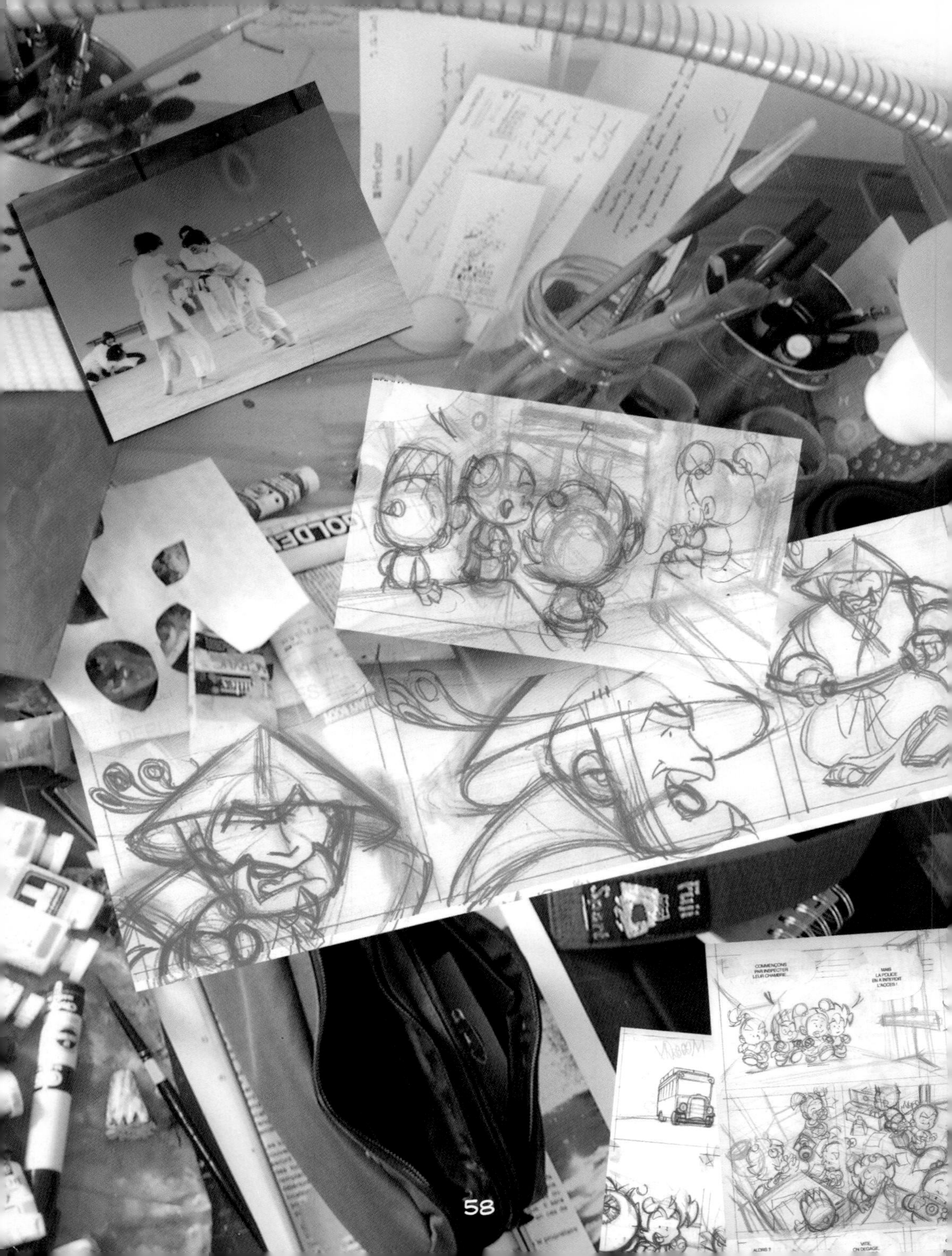
COMMENÇONS PAR INSPECTER LEUR CHAMBRE...
MAIS LA POLICE EN A INTERDIT L'ACCES !

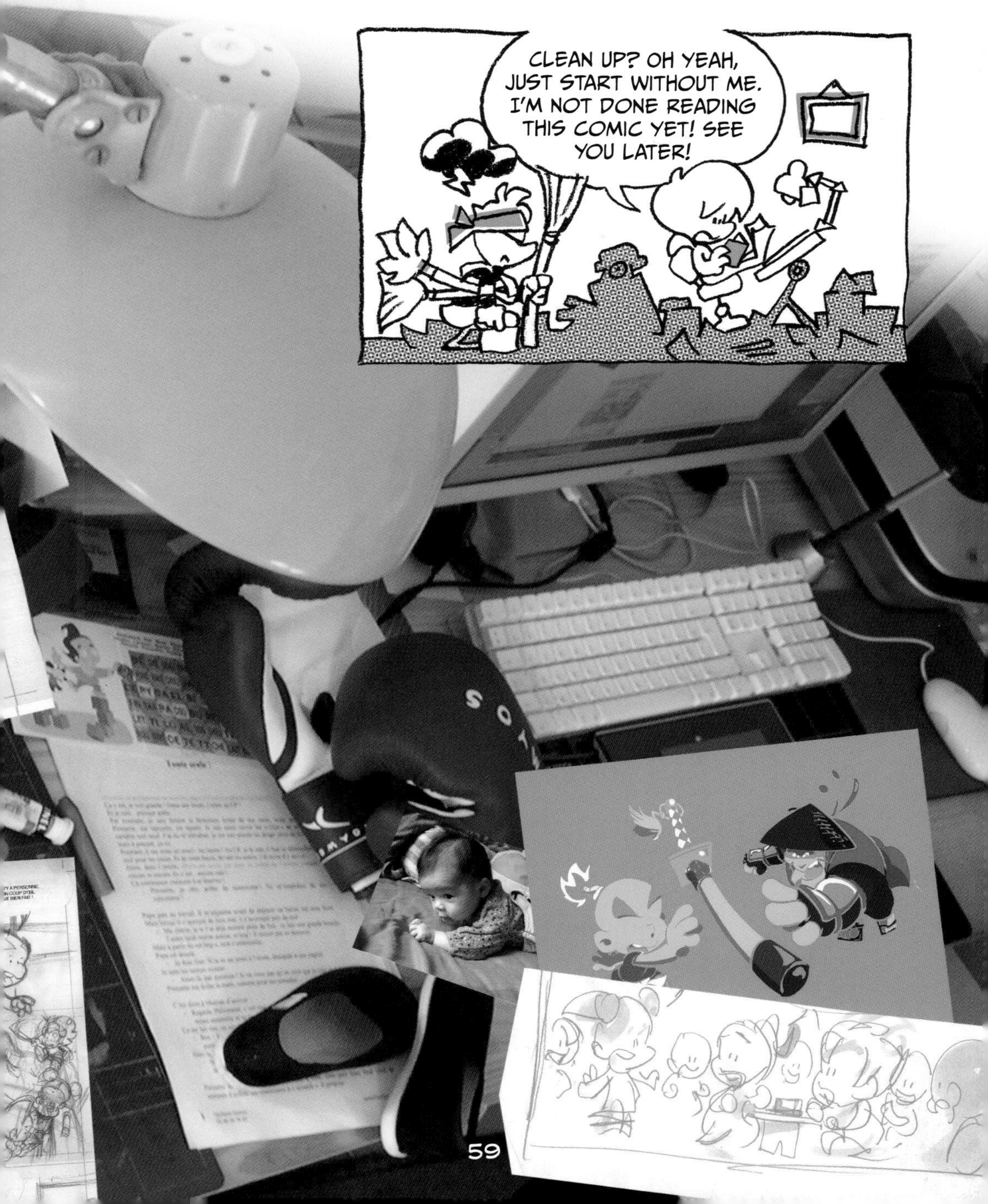
CLEAN UP? OH YEAH, JUST START WITHOUT ME. I'M NOT DONE READING THIS COMIC YET! SEE YOU LATER!

ABOUT THE AUTHOR

Laurent Richard worked in the world of advertising before becoming a professor of graphic arts. He now divides his time between teaching and illustration for children's publishing and media.

ABOUT THE ILLUSTRATOR

Nicolas Ryser attended the school of Graphic Arts Estienne in Paris. He won several competitions including the Angoulême and works for the magazine *Casus Belli*. He was recently awarded a *Graine de pro* ("Seed of a professional") prize.

TAO
The Little Samurai

#1 Pranks and Attacks!
#2 Ninjas and Knock Outs!
#3 Clowns and Dragons!
#4 The Championship!
#5 Wild Animals!